PENGUIN BOOKS

For the Love of Cupidity

Raven Kennedy is a California girl born and raised, whose love for books pushed her into creating her own worlds. The Plated Prisoner Series, a dark fantasy romance, has already sold in over a dozen countries and is a #1 international bestseller with over 1 million copies sold to date. It was inspired by the myth of King Midas and a woman's journey with finding her own strength. Her debut series was a romcom fantasy about a cupid looking for love of her own. She has since gone on to write in a range of genres. Whether she makes you laugh or cry, or whether the series is about a cupid or a gold-touched woman living in King Midas's gilded castle, she hopes to create characters that readers can root for. The Plated Prisoner series is being adapted for series by Peter Guber's Mandalay Television.

T0332762

FOR THE LOVE OF CUPIDITY

A VALENTINE'S DAY NOVELLA

RAVEN KENNEDY

PENGUIN BOOKS

PENGUIN BOOKS

UK | USA | Canada | Ireland | Australia
India | New Zealand | South Africa

Penguin Books is part of the Penguin Random House group of companies
whose addresses can be found at global.penguinrandomhouse.com

Penguin
Random House
UK

First published in the United States of America by Raven Kennedy 2019
First published in Great Britain by Penguin Books 2023
001

Copyright © Raven Kennedy, 2019

The moral right of the author has been asserted

Edited by Polished Perfection
Printed and bound in Great Britain by Clays Ltd, Elcograf S.p.A.

The authorized representative in the EEA is Penguin Random House Ireland,
Morrison Chambers, 32 Nassau Street, Dublin D02 YH68

A CIP catalogue record for this book is available from the British Library

ISBN: 978–1–405–96082–3

AUTHOR'S NOTE

This is a Valentine's Day novella, and is a continuation of the Heart Hassle series. This story takes place after the end of book three.
There is mature language and sexually explicit scenes. Intended for audiences 18 years and older.

To my amazing readers—this one is just for you.

CHAPTER 1

"*Y*ou're glowing again."

I crack open one eye and groan at being woken up.

"Deal with it," I mumble into the pillow.

I feel one of my mates pick up my wrist where my cupid boss mark is glowing bright pink. At first, I think he's about to lovingly caress it, but no. He shoves it under the blankets to snuff out the bright light.

Jerk.

"Too early," I hear Evert grumble, his voice all scratchy with sleep.

I agree, so I close my eyes again, ready to fall back into the heavy sleep that I'd been in, when there's a sudden screech that sounds like a banshee being tickled to pieces. A tiny body launches itself onto our bed, landing on one of the guys. I hear Sylred expel an oomph, and then the delighted screeching turns to incessant talking.

"Wake up, wake up, wake up! It's wing day!"

I lift up my head to find our two-year-old daughter sitting on Sylred's back while she shakes Ronak's muscled arm and flicks Evert's face with her red genfin tail. "Come on, Daddies! Wing day! Wing day!"

"Good gods, it's not even sunrise yet," Evert says, trying to bat away the tail in his face.

"You said if I went to sleep last night in my own bed, then today you'd teach me to fly. You said that."

I blame myself for her excellent speaking skills at such a young age. It's a blessing and a curse. She's been talking in full sentences since before her first birthday. She even talks in her sleep.

"I don't think you're gonna get them up this early," I tell her.

Amorette frowns in thought, and when none of the guys move, she stands up on Sylred's back and starts systematically hopping from genfin to genfin like they're stepping stones.

"That's one way to do it."

Before our boisterous daughter can hop onto Ronak for the third time, his arm shoots out, and he snags her around the middle and tosses her up into the air. She shrieks in delight.

My heart jumps at the ridiculous height her little body reaches, but that's always the case with these two. He catches her securely around her middle again and again, and she giggles joyfully. His impressive bicep flexes every time he tosses her up. Seriously, this guy has the best muscles ever. Sometimes I ask him to open jars or cut wood or lift something, even when I don't really need him to. I just like to watch his muscles flex. The sight makes my vaggie patch bloom.

"Again, again!" Amorette squeals, and her laughter is so infectious that I can't help but smile into my pillow.

"You females are so demanding," Ronak says, cocking a brown brow at me.

I lick my dry lips. "We just know what we want."

He catches Amorette one last time and then gets out of bed, swinging her up and over his shoulders so she can have a piggy back ride. "Wing time?"

"Yeah, wing time!" she says excitedly, her tail flicking behind her. Her tail is adorable. It's red like her wings with a little tuft of pink hair at the end that matches the ringlets on her head.

Ronak smacks Evert on the head as he passes. "You heard her. Get up. It's wing time."

"Fucking asshole," Evert grumbles, chucking a pillow at him.

"Daddy Ev! You said a bad word!" Amorette scolds.

"Yes, he did," Sylred says as he sits up from the bed. "And now he has to put more money in the jar." Sylred gets way too much enjoyment by making Evert pay up.

"Fucking jar," Evert grumbles as he sits up and scrubs his hands down his face.

Amorette points at him. "You said a bad word again!"

A laugh escapes me. Evert is forever in debt to the swear jar.

The guys toss Amorette to one another as they pull on shirts, and being the daredevil that she is, she giggles gleefully every time she's tossed around like a beachball.

With ringlets of pink hair and red-feathered wings like me, she's so cute that I can't help but smile every time I look at her. She looks like me, but there's no doubt that she takes after her genfin daddies, too, and I don't just mean the tail.

"Wait! I need my sword!"

She hops out of Evert's arms and goes racing out of the

room in search of her favorite toy. Yeah, a sword. Sylred made it for her out of wood, and she carries it around with her *everywhere*. She even sleeps with the thing. Ronak is oddly proud about it. He's also been sneaking off to teach her how to use it. He thinks I haven't noticed.

"You need anything?" Sylred asks, coming around to plant a kiss on my head.

"I'm good," I tell him with a smile. "Watch her, though. Ronak gets too crazy. Don't let him just drop her from the sky. I don't want her to be scared."

Sylred chuckles, but Ronak scoffs. "Our daughter is fearless."

"Okay, fine. But don't encourage that fearlessness too much. I don't want her getting hurt during her first flying lesson. She's brave, but sometimes she's too brave for her own good."

Ronak comes stalking toward me, and even though he has a shirt on now, the fabric still strains over his bulging muscles. I'm tempted to run my hands up his abs and pecs.

"I would never let anything happen to our daughter," he says, looking down at me sternly. He has his hot alpha voice on, and by the smug look on his face, he knows how much that tone gets to me. I shift my thighs together, wondering if I can possibly steal him away for a few minutes, but then Amorette comes sprinting into the room, and all my thoughts of a quickie go out the window.

We have to sneak off for sex nowadays. There's a system. It's a lot like passing the baton, but in our case, we pass a toddler to one of the guys while the rest of the guys sneak me out for a little hurried hoopty. They consider it a challenge to see who can make me orgasm the quickest.

4

"I'm ready!" Amorette says, wooden sword in hand. The thing is as tall as she is.

I smile. "Can I have a kiss first?"

She comes bounding over, little lips puckered as she lands one on my cheek. "Morning, Mommy!"

"Good morning, baby."

Excited, she grabs Sylred's and Ronak's hands and starts pulling them away. "Come on!"

"Be careful!" I call as the four of them disappear out of the room to go start her promised flying lessons.

I snuggle back under the covers, happy to get a few more minutes of blessed sleep, but of course, that's when I get the urgent need to pee.

With a defeated sigh, I throw the covers off. "Damn you, bladder."

Okot comes strolling in then, his bright red mohawk wet and slicked back from bathing. I smell his spicy scent mixed with the pine needle soap that Sylred makes.

When I bring my feet over the edge of the bed, he comes forward and takes my hand, helping me up.

As soon as I'm vertical, I huff out a breath like I just ran a marathon. "Getting out of bed is hard," I say.

Okot smiles and rests his large hands on my hugely pregnant belly. I look down at it and shake my head. "I was not this big with Amorette. It's got to be your fault that I look like I'm growing a baby who's part giant."

He runs his palm over my belly button, caressing me with both adoration and awe. I'll never get sick of that. Under his touch, the baby kicks, making both of us smile. "That was a strong one," he muses.

"Gets stronger every minute. It's like he or she is practicing kickboxing in there."

"I'll make you breakfast, my beloved."

My stomach grumbles at the mere suggestion. "Mmm food. Yes, please."

"Same thing as yesterday?" he asks.

I nod. "Yeah, but can I have extra garlic on the toast? And maybe some lime slices? Oh, and one of those eclairs. But not the cream-filled one."

He nods, not even blinking at my strange food requests as he moves to help me down the hallway.

I shuffle inside to the toilet and pee, and the relief is so intense that it makes me shiver. Peeing is such an event when pregnant. I feel like my whole life revolves around my bladder these days. I even have to plan ahead of time for it. We want to go somewhere? Gotta pee before we leave. We get there? Have to use the bathroom. About to leave? Nope, I need to go sit on the toilet first. Even if I don't feel like I need to pee, it's a bold, bladder-faced lie. I sit down on the toilet, and pee comes out regardless.

I pee day and night, and am constantly in a state of *Oh my gods, I need to go, or I'm gonna wet my pants.* It's all very hectic. It really keeps the guys on their toes, too. The moment we get somewhere, they're in a panic, making sure they find a toilet ASAP. I would laugh...except that would probably make me pee.

CHAPTER 2

*W*hen I'm done relieving my bladder, Okot comes in and draws the bath for me, testing the temperature several times until he's confident that it's not too hot or too cold. He even pours in the lemon-scented soap that I like. I can't use the lavender one anymore. If I catch one whiff, my gag reflex goes on high alert.

Okot gently removes my nightdress, and even though I'm as big as a boulder, he gathers me into his arms and lowers me into the water. It's one of the rules in the house now that I'm so big. I had one too many near falls getting my fat ass into the tub, so one of them makes sure to always help me in.

Once I'm safely submerged, Okot leaves me to go prepare my breakfast. They learned when I was pregnant with Amorette that my voracious appetite didn't slow down, but it did get a bit weirder.

I can't reach my toes, or even my knees, so I just sort of flop a washcloth down over the general area and hope the soaking gets me clean enough.

Okot comes in a while later to help me out. After drying me off, he has me sit on the bench in front of the vanity. My genfins made everything in this entire den by hand, and the bathroom is one of my favorite rooms. Aside from the gorgeous tub, the window looks out onto the flower box. There's just enough sunlight coming in to make the white-gray marble sparkle.

Naked, I sit on the bench and watch as Okot squeezes oil onto his hands and picks up my foot to start rubbing the oil into my skin. He works quietly and slowly, his large, callused hands working the oil into the arches of my swollen feet, up my calves and thighs, down my arms, and adding delicious pressure into my shoulders and aching back before finishing with my belly.

It's both relaxing and a turn-on. I don't know whether I want to take a nap or jump him.

But really, why choose? I could totally do both.

I reach forward and take a fistful of his shirt, yanking him down and slamming his lips against mine. His septum piercing tickles my nose as I shift my head, my tongue flicking against his. A low sound of approval hums in his chest, and his hand comes up to surround my neck, the pad of his thumb dancing across my throat in a featherlight touch.

"Your breakfast will get cold," he says against my lips, his red-ringed eyes pulsing with desire. I freaking love that look.

"Don't care," I say, pulling him back to me, needing his lips on mine. "I can reheat the limes."

He obliges, nipping and sipping at my bottom lip, catching it between his teeth and pulling just enough to sting deliciously.

When his oiled fingers trail down to my core and

8

graze over my clit, I make a super embarrassing keening noise that I just can't stop.

While keeping pressure on my nub, he slips two fingers inside of me, and I lose my grasp on his shirt. When I start to tip back, Okot slips his arms around me and hauls me up to my feet. I immediately brace my hands on the counter and push my ass out. It's one of the only sex positions I'm still awesome at when I'm this pregnant, and the guys don't complain one bit.

Okot loosens the ties of his pants and then drops them to his ankles. I watch in the mirror as his huge penis pops out like a jack-in-the-box. And just like with a jack-in-the-box, it both thrills me and scares me a little. His piercings glint in the light, and I lick my lips in anticipation.

"Gods, you're so freaking big. I still can't believe you manage to fit that thing inside of me without ripping me in half."

"I would never hu—"

His words cut off, and I look at him in the mirror's reflection. My eyes soften when I see his expression. I know that look. He's remembering when his mind was being controlled and he attacked me. He's remembering how he hurt me.

His eyes drop to my throat, as if he's seeing his hands wrapped around it, choking the air out of me. It's gotten better with time, but the memories still haunt him.

I pick up his hand and slowly lift it. His eyes snap to mine in the mirror as I deliberately put his hand back around my throat. He needs to be reminded that I trust him. He needs to be shown that I know he'd never hurt me. Hopefully, if I remind him enough, he'll eventually trust himself again.

His hand is tense and still for a moment, but when I

reach back behind me and slowly begin to stroke his length, he finally relaxes. His hand at my throat cradles me gently, his thumb rubbing up and down my sensitive skin as I work him in my hand. He's so big my fingers don't touch.

Okot lines up behind me and traces his hand over the curve of my butt before moving my hair off my back and leaning into the crook of my neck. He breathes in slowly, like he's drinking in my scent, and I feel his already huge erection grow even bigger. I drop my hand from him as he grinds against me, and when he flicks his tongue out to taste the skin of my neck, I'm so turned on that I have to take matters into my own hands. I let my hand drop between my thighs and start playing with myself, and Okot groans at the sight.

"Please," I tell him, my voice husky.

But instead of entering me, Okot drops to his knees, grips my thighs, and starts eating me out from behind.

"OhmygodsIwasnotexpectingthat."

Okot is big everywhere. Even his tongue is big. So when he lays it flat and licks my slit, I nearly jump ten feet in the air, and probably would have if he wasn't holding me so securely. His thick, wet tongue pushes into me, and my lamassu freaking *worships* me with it, licking, sipping, and just generally giving me the best tongue-fuck I've ever had. And I have four mates who like to take a lot of trips down south, so that's saying a lot.

I clench my eyes tight when I come, his name falling from my lips and bouncing off the walls. With my pussy still rippling with the orgasm, Okot stands and starts pushing into me, the huge head of his cock slowly breaching me.

So careful not to hurt me, he goes agonizingly slow,

pushing in inch by inch. My body compensates for his girth, and I breathe in, forcing myself to relax until he pushes all the way in.

When I feel the front of his thighs touch me, I breathe out a sigh of relief. "Oh gods, I did it. It's all the way in," I say victoriously in a garbled tone.

Okot laughs in his low, gravelly tone of his that I love. "You always say that."

"Well, have you seen your penis? You'd give yourself a pat on the back if you managed it, too. It's like a freaking beluga whale."

"I...don't know what that is."

"Big sea thing," I pant.

With another laugh, he starts slowly moving inside of me, and I watch us in the mirror, his body about double the width of mine even with my huge belly hanging down. I love that I can still feel small with Okot, even when I'm this huge. And I am freaking huge. My boobs have blown up like balloons, and my ass puffed up like a baked cake. The guys love it though, so there's that.

Okot takes me slowly, his pierced cock rubbing that perfect spot inside of me until I'm begging all sorts of unintelligible things, writhing against him as I continue to touch myself. If he keeps this up, he'll probably fuck me right into labor.

When I come again, the orgasm is intense, spreading through me from head to toe until I become jelly in his arms. He pushes his hips up hard, buries his face against my neck, and finds his own release with the sexiest damn groan in the world.

Totally spent, I flop my head and arms onto the counter, but my belly is seriously heavy hanging down like this, so I grudgingly go upright again with Okot's

11

help. When my legs shake a bit, Okot laughs and kisses me sweetly on the lips. Keeping a firm hold on my arms, he uses a towel to clean us both off, and then he lowers a dress over me and starts doing up the ties.

"You're so sweet to me," I tell him, my eyes still shining with that post-orgasmic bliss.

"You are my beloved," he says, like that explains everything.

And maybe it does.

CHAPTER 3

When we finally make our way out of the bathroom, dawning sunlight kisses the sky, bathing our den in a lavender glow.

Sitting at the table, Okot serves me up my breakfast, which I inhale in about two-point-seven minutes.

I'm wiping my lips on a cloth napkin when the rest of my family comes barreling in from outside.

"Mommy! I flew! I flew!"

She races up to me, hopping up and down on her bare feet excitedly.

I beam, watching as her curls bounce with her movement, her cheeks flushed with excitement and the kiss of cool air outside.

"Already?" I ask, impressed. "That was fast."

She runs over to Okot next, who's at the stove cooking everyone else a "normal" breakfast, as they call it. I really don't know why they refuse to eat the limes and garlic toast. It's delicious.

"Daddy! Did you hear? I flew!"

Okot sets the utensil down and lifts her up. "I did hear.

I am very proud of you," he says, his voice filled with pride.

I swear, every time I see my mates with our daughter, my ovaries start to throb. When we first had Amorette, I was worried that there would be jealousy, but that hasn't been the case at all. It was never even an issue of exactly *which* genfin is her biological father, and Okot doesn't see her as any less his just because she has a genfin tail. In their eyes, they're all her daddies, and they work together as a perfect unit. Of course, she's had them wrapped around her little red tail since birth.

She climbs up Okot's arms to his shoulders. "Yep! I did this!" she says, spreading out her arms and red wings. "Daddy Ro frew me in the air, and I fly-falled. Daddy Ev catched me."

I shoot a look at Sylred, and he scratches the back of his neck sheepishly. "They were being careful."

"Then, Daddy Ev let me climb on the roof and jump off!"

None of my genfins will look me in the eye after that one.

"Is that so?" I ask dryly. I'm not even surprised, to be honest.

"Let's eat before you get the genfins into any more trouble," Okot tells her, his eyes sparkling with amusement.

Amorette climbs down, and Okot starts loading everyone up with pancakes, which I politely decline. Pancakes for breakfast? Gross.

I get up to pee again, and when I toddle back, I notice my cupid boss mark start glowing.

"Again?" Sylred says, tilting his head at my arm when I return.

"Yeah…"

My mates all shoot me looks that I promptly pretend to be oblivious of.

"You said you'd take time off," Sylred reminds me.

"I know, but I can't just leave them hanging."

Guilt claws at me. Now that I know more about my cupid boss powers, I know that my mark starts glowing whenever there's an issue in Cupidville.

The only problem? I can't actually *go* to Cupidville. Firstly, because I'm pregnant, and we don't know how that will affect the baby. Secondly, we can't have Ronak turning feral and not being able to snap out of his animal state.

I've been working remotely when an issue crops up. Usually, that's okay, because I can call Sev here and delegate to him. But the mark has been glowing more incessantly lately, and Sev isn't the most reliable or the most driven. He gets distracted by his dick a lot. Honestly, we're probably two of the worst cupids in existence. And we're in charge. It's been a long three years.

"Why don't you take care of whatever it is that they need this time, and then tell them you're on a break until the baby comes," Sylred suggests.

"Yes, my beloved. We want you relaxed," Okot adds.

"I'm totally relaxed," I insist as I bite my nails.

"You barely sleep more than two hours at a time," Ronak rumbles, looking displeased.

"That's just because I have to get up to pee."

"You keep a pile of heart-shaped cupid paperwork shoved in the pantry, and you sneak in there to work when you think we aren't looking," Sylred says.

"Umm…I'm just getting snacks?"

They roll their eyes.

"You're scratching. A lot. Which you always do when you're stressed," Evert says, looking pointedly at my hand that's…yep, it's scratching my old itch. Dammit.

I throw my hands up in frustration. "I can't help it! I'm the boss. I have to, like, do stuff."

"How about asking Lex to help?" Sylred suggests.

My stomach plummets at the thought of Lex, and I immediately start to shake my head. "She's not my assistant anymore, you know that."

"Yeah, but you haven't accepted another assistant, either. Besides, I'm sure she could help," Sylred tells me gently.

I sip on some spiced buttermilk that Okot made for me, watching as the five of them devour a huge stack of pancakes.

"I know," I say, looking down at my mug and picking at grains in the wooden table. "I just…I know it hurts her to come here. She tries to put on a good front, but I can tell. Plus, I can feel it. Her heartbreak. It makes me feel so bad, because it was my f—"

"Don't say it was your fault. The Horned Hook's death was *not* your fault." Evert glares at me. "The prince attacked, and Belren chose to take the hit."

It most decidedly *was* my fault, but this is an argument I'll never win. We've had it for years.

I sigh. "I don't want to make her keep reliving it."

Ronak leans back, placing his arm over the back of my chair and toys with the ends of my pink hair. "It's been three years," he points out.

"Yeah, and she's still not okay," I remind him. "She changed after Belren took the blast that would've hit her. I thought things would get better with time, but now I'm thinking that she'll never be the same."

Amorette's eyes bounce between us from her wooden highchair. "Whatcha talkin' about?" she asks around a mouthful of food.

"Don't talk and chew," Sylred reprimands, directing her attention away from our conversation by launching into the importance of keeping her wings clean.

Ronak's attention moves back to me. "Then maybe she doesn't need time. Maybe she needs something else to keep her mind off it."

I shake my head. "Not yet. I'll let her be for a while longer."

"Well, you've got to do *something*, because you're working too much. That mark is gonna keep glowing at all hours of the day and night unless you get a better handle on things," Evert says.

Damn meddling mates. I'd argue more...if they weren't right.

Not that I'll tell them that.

CHAPTER 4

*J*ust thinking of all the crap I'll probably be bombarded with is enough to make me want to crawl back into bed. I also don't want to tell the cupids that I need a break, but the pointed looks from my mates let me know that they aren't going to let me put this off.

"Fine, I'll tell them I can work this one last time, but then I'm gonna take a week off after the baby is born."

"Twelve weeks," Evert counters.

"Are you insane? I can't take twelve weeks off. I'm the freaking boss!"

"Ten," Ronak says.

"Three," I retaliate.

"Nine," Sylred offers.

These guys are freaking relentless. "Four. I'll do a whole month. That's a lot," I say, trying to convince them.

The guys all exchange a look, and then Okot leans forward and picks up my hand. The gesture is sweet and makes me relax a bit from being ganged-up on. He strokes

19

the pad of his finger over my palm, softening me immediately. "Take eight weeks, my beloved."

I smile dreamily at him. "Okay."

My genfins blink in surprise, but Okot just smiles and leans back, looking proud.

"What the fuck? Why did you agree to him so fast?" Evert demands.

"Daddy said a bad word again!" Amorette giggles.

"Because. She was *taken care of* by him this morning," Sylred says pointedly.

Sex code talk in front of a toddler has become a necessity.

Evert rolls his eyes. "Well, then we should've let the fucking lamassu open up the debate. She would've folded at twelve weeks right off the bat."

"I would not have," I argue. I probably would have.

Evert gives me a look. "You always cave to whoever...*took care of you* last."

I shrug. Okay, fine. He's not wrong.

"Well, eight weeks. That's the deal," I say, taking another sip of buttermilk. Sniffing it slightly, I reach for the salt and pepper and dump some in. Swishing it around, I take another drink and sigh in contentment. Much better.

When my cupid boss mark starts glowing more brightly, my mates give me sharp looks.

"Fine! I'll call Sev and tell him."

"Ooh! Can I play with Sev? He talks funny," Amorette says excitedly.

"Absolutely not," Evert says, standing and plucking her from her seat.

Her bottom lip pokes out. "Why not?"

"Because he's a fucking terrible influence."

Yeah, the irony is not lost on me.

"Daddy said a bad word again!"

"Sorry!" Evert barks, warding off all of our exasperated looks as he ducks out of the kitchen with a sticky Amorette in tow.

"Take care of it, little demon. Today," Ronak says in his bossy tone, which he softens by using his draped arm to pull me close and land a kiss to the top of my head.

Then he stands and follows Evert out, while Sylred starts clearing the table. I get up to help him, but he shakes his head. "No. Sit."

"I can help," I insist. "I'm pregnant, not an invalid."

"The last time you started helping with the dishes, you started dry heaving," he points out.

"Yeah, well...as long as there aren't any gross food particles stuck to any of the plates, I can totally do the dishes."

He cocks a blond brow, the corner of his lip tilting up. "I'm pretty sure our dirty food plates are going to have food on them."

"Fine. Then I'll wipe the table," I say, moving to grab the rag.

But the moment I pick it up, Okot reaches out and grips it. I don't want to let it go, though, so we have a weird, super mellow tug-of-war contest before he gently peels my latched-on fingers from the rag and takes it from me.

"When you wiped the table down two days ago, you started crying," he gently reminds me.

I huff out an annoyed breath. "That's because I found a moisture ring stained into the wood! It was upsetting!"

"Wasn't it just—"

I cut him off. "Yes, it just ended up being syrup. But still. It *could have* been a moisture ring."

Now both of them are trying not to laugh at me.

"Fine. I'll just go sweep."

They exchange a look. I can see it in their faces. They want to argue *again*, but they're the nice ones, so they just shuffle awkwardly on their feet and make things weird.

I clench my teeth. "*What?*"

"It's just...well, umm..." A red blush creeps over Sylred's cheeks as he trails off.

"Just say it! Why can't I freaking sweep?"

Ronak comes walking in, heading for his mug that he'd left behind. "Because your belly is so big that the broom handle runs into it, and you can't see your feet, so you end up missing what little dirt you *do* manage to get."

He walks back out before I can reply. I feel a kick, like the baby is agreeing with him. Not cool.

"Yeah? Well..." Not having even a semblance of a comeback, I trail off, and the front door shuts behind a chuckling Ronak. "Asshole alpha," I grumble.

I eye Sylred and Okot, who have suddenly become *very* busy with cleaning. So busy, in fact, that they're avoiding my looks.

Cowards.

"Fine. I guess I'll just go into the front room and do cupid stuff," I say, nearly pouting.

Sylred turns and nods with a relieved look on his face. "Good. It's better to get it all taken care of before the baby comes. Which should be any day now, judging by your, umm, size..."

He blinks, a horrified look coming over his face as he realizes what he just said.

"What's wrong with my size?"

"Nothing," he says quickly. Too freaking quickly.

"Are you saying I'm fat?"

Sylred makes a choking sound like he's suffocating on his own stupid words and hurriedly shakes his head. "No, no, no. That's not what I'm saying. I wouldn't say that."

My eyes narrow on him. "You wouldn't say that? So then, it's true, but you just *wouldn't say it*, because you're too nice? Is that it? Is that what you're saying?"

His brown eyes widen. "I, umm, you…ahhh…what?"

"My beloved."

Okot's voice cuts through the super hormonal haze of anger, and I realize that my hands are smoking. Anger always sets off my wonky demon powers. Go figure. As soon as my gaze flicks to the lamassu, Sylred slinks away, practically running toward the sink.

Okot moves in front of me and touches my belly. "Take a deep breath, my beloved."

I do, and the hellish smoke dissipates.

"Now listen," he says, grasping my neck. "You are beautiful. You are round with our child, looking like a goddess. We do not think you are fat, because you aren't, and even if you were, you would still be beautiful to us. Understand?"

I slowly nod, the last of the irrational anger expelling out of me as he trails his thumb over my bottom lip. He just gave me two orgasms not even an hour ago, so I sort of just melt at everything he says and does.

"Good," he says, placing a kiss on my forehead. "Now, go take care of your cupid work, and let them know about taking time off. When you are finished, I will rub your feet."

I find myself turning around and walking out of the kitchen. I can't resist a good foot rub.

23

CHAPTER 5

When I'm settled on the cushioned couch, I take a deep breath and rub at the cupid boss mark before calling Sev's name.

He appears in a cloud of pink, and I open my mouth to say hello, only to stop short.

"Hey—Why are you naked? *Again?*" I ask as I slap a hand over my eyes.

"Fooking right, are you mad in it? Always the worst shite timing, boss."

"Mates!"

My yell brings all four of my mates inside, and then there's a lot of cursing.

"What the fuck? Why is your dick pointing at my mate?" Evert growls.

"She fooking called me right in the middle of me pokin' the fud, get it? I weren't finished!" Sev defends, his hands clasped over his junk.

I hear a sigh. "Syl, go get the cupid some damn pants," Ronak orders.

25

Only after Sylred returns, and I hear Sev pulling on clothes, do I remove the hand from in front of my eyes.

I try to cross my arms in front of me, but my belly is really sticking out, so I end up just pushing my enormous boobs together.

Evert, of course, latches onto the view and doesn't look away, even after I drop my arms. He's been very appreciative of my extra-large boobs that I've gained during pregnancy and never misses an opportunity to ogle them.

When he finally raises his blue eyes to meet mine, I shoot him a flirtatious wink. His gaze instantly goes hungry, and he coughs out some wayward Lust while fixing the front of his pants.

When he sees me shift on the couch and press my legs together, he smirks, making a dimple pop out on his cheek behind the black scruff on his jaw.

If I could get off this couch without help, I'd totally jump him right now.

"If you don't stop looking at me like that, I'll be forced to take you back to our bedroom," he growls.

I reach out my hands. "Sounds great. Someone help me up."

Sylred laughs. "No. You called Sev so you could do whatever Cupidville needs, remember? You can have sex after."

"Don't be a right fooking radge. If she wants to fook, I'll be happy to wait and watch," he says with a wink.

Ronak and Evert both growl.

"Too far," I mumble to Sev.

"Where's Amorette?" I ask, looking at my mates. "So help me, Ronak, if you left her on the roof..."

"Relax, she's with the gardener. She's helping him prune."

"You mean she's digging up all of our flowers."

"Probably."

"Alright." I clap. "Everyone who isn't a cupid, go do... whatever it is you were doing, while I talk to Sev."

My mates leave but not before Evert comes up to me, letting his tail trail across my thighs. "I'll be in as soon as he leaves, Scratch," he says with a hungry promise.

My heart flutters in my chest, and I nod, thinking about all of the hot, naughty sex things we can do. Then he walks out, leaving me in a puddle of need, and Sev arches a brow at the serious lust waves I'm giving off right now.

"Good fooking grief, boss. Get a handle on it, yeah? You're making my tadger stiff again."

I wrinkle my nose. "Don't talk about your stiffies."

He just shrugs.

"Okay," I say, getting down to business. "Lay it on me. What's going on in Cupidville? This thingy won't stop glowing."

He sits down on the chair opposite me, propping his ankles up on the table. "It's a right fooking mess, boss."

"Why?"

This cupid boss business is harder than I thought it would be. Keeping Love Matches sorted, Love Arrow manufacturing, running the still fairly new HR department, not to mention keeping each of the Veil Major and Minor representatives happy. Plus, there's all of the day-to-day cupid stuff. It's...a lot. And since I can't even go to Cupidville, that means delegating a lot of things out.

Unfortunately, all of the delegating has fallen on Sev's shoulders. And let's face it, he's pretty, but he's a terrible manager. But I can't bear to ask Lex to help. The last time I saw her, she still couldn't look me in the eye, and then she asked to be sent to the troll realm. But it was when she lost her status as Cupid of the Month that I knew things were really bad. Trouble is, I don't know how to help her. Ever since Belren died for her, she's just been... disconnected. So that means Sev and I have to handle this on our own. I can't dump more on poor Lex right now.

"We keep getting' a fuck ton of recruits," Sev says, breaking me out of my thoughts.

I blink at him. "What?"

"Recruits, aye? New cupid shitheads. Everyone in the Veil won't shut their right dirty traps, get it? They go on and on about our new cupid benefits, and then the second-lifers start lining up to get their red wings. We're overrun, boss. Can't train 'em fast enough, not since you're the one who made training mandatory."

I pinch the bridge of my nose. "The reports show that new cupids are doing a much better job during their first year since I've created the training program," I point out a tad defensively.

Sev holds his hands up in surrender. "I ain't saying it's a bad thing, boss. I'm just saying we're fooking behind. Especially for the Earth realm. Bloody Valentine's Day is next week, and that realm is so overdue on Love Matches, it ain't even funny. If we don't get these new arseholes trained up in time for Valentine's, we'll be so behind we won't be able to dig ourselves out for another fooking year at least. We're doin' the best we can, get it? But there's one group of trainees that keep fooking failing."

"Failing? How can they be failing? Training isn't even hard."

28

Sev shrugs. "The little shites are the worst cupids I've ever seen."

Coming from Sev, that's saying something.

"Dammit." I blow out a stressed-filled breath and rub my belly.

Sev grimaces slightly at the sight. "That thing is really fooking big."

My hand goes still as I glare at him. Apparently, my glare doesn't work on him nearly as well as it does on my mates, because he just shrugs. "Your diddies look fooking great, though."

My glare instantly turns into a beam as I look down at my ample chest. "Thank you! They really are impressive, aren't they? Evert likes them."

Sev nods. "Aye. Fooking glorious."

"He'd better not be talking about your fucking tits!" Evert's voice comes hollering through the open window.

Then Amorette's voice, "What's a tits?"

We aren't going to be winning any parenting awards anytime soon, that's for sure.

"Okay. We can deal with this," I say, although I'm pretty sure I'm trying to convince myself more than I'm trying to convince Sev. "I'll just have to get super boss bitch on them. Scare them straight, kind of thing."

Sev looks at me, his perfect face betraying his doubt. "You sure you don't want to call number sixty-nine? She's a right smadge better at this cupid shite than us. No offense, boss."

"None taken," I reply. "But no. We've gotta deal with this on our own, Sev. And then I have to take a break. The baby will be here any day, and I promised my mates that I'd take eight weeks off."

He sighs and runs a hand over his borrowed shirt. It

fits a bit weird since it's one of Ronak's made to accommodate wings. But even though they have the same cupid wings, Sev is much, much smaller than Ronak, so he kind of swims in it. He's still pretty, though.

"Fooking hell. You didn't take that long of a break after the other one was born."

"Exactly. My mates never let me hear the end of it."

He blows out another breath. "Alright," Sev finally says, conceding. He looks super disappointed that he'll actually have to work.

"Since I still can't physically get to Cupidville, I'm going to have to work from home. I guess...you'll just have to bring the surplus of cupid recruits here."

He arches a brow. "Here?"

I nod. "Yep. I'll just train them here in the fae realm."

"No offense, *again*, but do you actually know how to train these pink shiteheads?"

"I can totally handle it."

He gives me another look but then shrugs. "What about your mates? They gonna shite themselves?"

Probably. "Nah. They'll understand."

Sev doesn't look convinced, but he doesn't push the matter. "Want me to bring 'em now?"

"Yeah, let's do this..." I pause, making a face. "Right after I pee."

See? The peeing thing. It's a problem.

CHAPTER 6

When I'm done in the bathroom, I walk back to the front room, only to stumble to a halt at the sight of a dozen cupids now stuffed inside. The room suddenly feels tiny.

Even though Sev warned me that these cupids failed training once before, it didn't really sink in until just now. Because now that they're in front of me, I can kind of see why.

They're a motley crew of cupids. Leather jackets, goth makeup, hipsters, nerds, a couple weird-looking fae, and one chick is wearing a ball gown like she was an actual princess. Another one has a cell phone stuck to her hand like she died mid-text. She keeps trying to scroll, even though it doesn't work anymore. There's even a damn troll cupid. A *troll*. He can barely fit inside without his head hitting my ceiling.

To put it simply, even with their new pink hair and red wings, they don't look like the cupid-type. I'm surprised as hell that they picked this as their afterlife job, to be honest.

I walk further into the room to stand beside Sev. "These are the trainees?"

He's schmoozing up some cupid beside him, taking advantage of their physical state by running a finger up her arm. She either has a fetish or she was at a costume party when she died, because her face is painted to look like a skull, and she's wearing some tight leather getup with assless chaps. What a time to die.

"Sev!" I snap, pinching him on the nipple when he continues to ignore me.

He rubs at his pec and gives me a glare. "Did you need something?"

"Yes! Help me," I whisper-yell.

There are entirely too many cupids staring at me right now, and I feel totally on the spot. They're intimidating. It's like I'm the teacher forced to run detention for all the slackers. I'm sensing an impending mutiny. Why did I think that I could do this?

"Just tell 'em how to blow Lust shite and shoot some arrows. They're fooking hopeless, though, so I wouldn't get too excited."

"Thanks for the positivity," I say dryly.

"You're the boss, so boss the shite out of these jobbies, or poof the fookers."

Turning, I march to the front of the room to address them. Well, I don't march, to be honest. I waddle.

"Okay, cupids," I say, addressing them. "It's nice to meet you, I'm Emelle." I flash them the inside of my wrist to show them my cupid number and boss mark. "Since you failed your last training, I'll be taking over."

They look at me, utterly bored. I'm pretty sure a couple in the back are making out. And...where did that one get a pipe to smoke?

"Okay, guys, pay attention," I say, clapping my hands. They don't pay attention.

"Hey, when's our break?" the troll cupid asks.

"Yeah, and when do we get to take vacation time?" another one pipes up.

That's it. I narrow my eyes, fluff up my wings, and let a bit of my angel power through so that I start to shine like a night-light. It's the only angel power I know how to use, but it looks impressive. "Hey!"

The cupids finally deign to look up at me.

"Listen up, I'm just gonna say it. You guys totally suck," I tell them. Sev starts laughing at their expense, and I earn some glares, but I push on. "But, if you can stop sucking and become decent cupids, you guys won't be in danger of getting poofed. If you want all the perks that come with the job, then you're gonna have to earn it."

"Yeah, and if you arseholes fail again, you're gettin' poofed for sure," Sev adds.

They grumble their unhappiness. "You guys picked this job, and you're stuck with it," I tell them. "So buck up, or I'll be forced to poof my first ever cupid, and I don't want to have to do that." I let the threat hang in the air for a beat. I don't know if I could actually terminate any of them, but the warning seems to work, and they look like they take me a bit more seriously. "You've all been assigned to the Earth realm, so we need to get you ready for Valentine's Day. We only have one week. Let's start with practicing some Flirt-Touches."

When no one moves, I glare at them in a super intimidating way. Or not. My dress is nearly bursting at the seams, I'm barefoot because my feet are too swollen for my shoes, and my hair looks like a hot mess.

For added effect, I snap my fingers and make the

terminate button appear. This makes them jump to it. I barely suppress a smirk. I'm totally boss bitching the eff out of them right now.

"Practice on each other. Skin-to-skin works best," I explain, demonstrating how the power should look and work as I swipe my finger across Sev's jugular. He gets a dopey look on his face. "Aww, luv. What say you and I go out and eat some food under the moonlight or some right soppy shite before we do the diddy?"

I arch a brow. "That's your idea of flirting?"

"Fooking right."

I turn back to the cupids. "Let's see it."

They break off and begin to practice, the room immediately filling with toying romance. The girl in the ball gown starts giggling, the goth guy is reciting lyrics from a rock metal band like it's Shakespeare, and cell phone girl begins talking in flirtatious hashtags.

Pretty soon, they're all loosened up, and I show them how to use the Flirt-Touches with some more finesse. Once they do a few more passes, they're not nearly as hopeless as I first thought. Once they actually *try*, they're just fine at it. For this group, motivation seems to be the key.

After practicing Flirt-Touches for an hour or so, I feel like I've worked plenty for one day. "Okay, everyone, I think that's good for today. Let's break and continue training tomorrow."

The cupids look around. "What should we do until then?"

"Umm..." Crap. What am I gonna do with all of them? I can't send them back to Cupidville because the time warp will throw things off. "I'll get you situated with somewhere to stay. Hang out in here until I get back." I pause. "But no having sex on my bed. Or my couch. Or my bathroom. Actually, just no sex whatsoever in here, got it?"

They look disappointed.

I shuffle out of the room and head outside to find my mates. I find Ronak first. He's out back, training as usual. He's lifting huge boulders and chucking them across the yard like they're pebbles, even though they shake the ground as they land. Ronak's muscles are bulging, his shirt is off, sweat is slicking down his tanned skin...and I'm horny again.

When he spots me, he tosses the boulder in his arms over his head—one-handed—like it's nothing. "Done already, little demon?"

Motioning toward my stomach, I say, "There is nothing little about me."

As soon as I'm closer, he snatches my hand and pulls me against him. I don't even mind the guy sweat, because now his abs and V are right in front of me, and that shit is just nice to look at.

"Not true," he says, raising my fingers in front of his face.

Very slowly, I watch as he raises my pinky up and then sucks it into mouth. My breath catches as his hot, wet tongue dances around it, his teeth scraping against it ever so slightly. When he drags my finger out of his mouth, his eyes stay locked on mine.

"This finger is still little," he says, his voice husky.

I swallow hard and nod. I don't even know what I'm nodding at, to be honest. I forgot what we were talking about as soon as my finger went into his mouth.

I don't notice that his tail has wrapped around my arm until I feel it tugging my hand toward the front of his

35

pants. My hand lands on his hard length, and the second I feel it beneath my palm, I feel my insides heat.

His hands move to cup my breasts over my dress, and he strums his thumbs against my nipples. "And then there's these little nipples. Pink and peaked and perfect."

His breath fans my neck when he leans in and scrapes his sharp canine against the curve of my neck. My lashes automatically flutter closed. His tail demands that I continue to pay attention to his cock though, so I squeeze him hard, just the way I know he likes it.

He growls low in his chest, and then his hand moves to cup me between my thighs, and if his other arm weren't holding me around the waist, I would've dropped right to the ground.

A whimper escapes me as he presses the heel of his palm against my throbbing clit, and I feel his smile against my neck.

"And this? This little pussy right here? It's the perfect size for my cock."

This time, my knees actually do buckle, but he simply just holds me against his chest, my feet not even touching the ground anymore. He does it while not smooshing me against him, either; ever mindful of my protruding belly, his hold is firm and steady, despite my body's awkward girth. And he does it all with one arm.

And...I orgasm. Just like that.

I try to hide it because...for fuck's sake that's just embarrassing, but Ronak rears back and looks at me. I'm still shaking from the orgasm, and I'm pretty sure I'm grimacing from trying to hold it in.

"Did...did you just come?"

"What? No," I say quickly. "That's ridiculous. People don't come by one stupid touch."

The asshole alpha smiles. "You *did*. You just came on my hand. I barely touched you."

"I did *not* just come. You're mistaken."

"I felt your pussy clench against my hand. Through your dress, even. And you forget, I can *always* scent it."

Godsdammit. He's gonna be so cocky now.

"Shut up," I tell him.

The asshole laughs.

"Fucking hell. You got her all worked up again? I can smell her need from here. And...did she come?"

I look over to see Evert, Sylred, and Okot walking up, all three pairs of nostrils flaring. How embarrassing.

Ronak nods, and his wings puff up. "Yep, after about three seconds."

"She gets worked up easily these days," Evert muses, although he looks happy about it.

"It's true," Sylred says. "Her panties get drenched at least once a day."

"You guys sexually tease me and get me all revved up!" I defend. "And I'm not *that* bad."

It's a bit awkward defending myself when I'm still hanging in Ronak's arm on account of being too horny to stand.

"I thought the fucking lamassu took care of your morning needs?" Evert asks.

My brows raise. "Are you guys keeping track?"

"We make sure our mate is sated," Sylred answers.

"So, you all talk about me when I'm not around? What, are you keeping a tally?"

"More like a schedule," Sylred admits.

I blink at them, unsure if I should be insulted or impressed at them for being so organized.

"I can stand now," I tell Ronak.

"If you want me to put you down, you're going to have to let go of my cock—*if* you can."

I look down between us, but...yeah, I can't see anything past my belly. I drop my hand that was, in fact, still squeezing his cock. "I did it," I say with more pride than I probably should.

CHAPTER 7

Once Ronak sets me down, I'm instantly reminded how freaking heavy it is to be upright on my own. I'm half tempted to ask him to pick me up again, but I resist. "Where's Amorette?"

"Well, much to our surprise, we went inside to get some lunch, only to find our den is filled with cupids," Sylred says, giving me a look. "She's playing with them and showing off her wings."

Ronak sighs. "Why is our den filled with cupids?"

"Oh, I just had to do some training," I say nonchalantly as I pick off some imaginary lint from my dress. "It's nearly Valentine's Day on Earth, you know. It's our busiest season. And Valentine's is important for us cupids. It's special."

Ronak narrows his eyes. "Did you finish training them? And did you tell Sev about the time off you're taking?" Sylred asks.

I fidget with my black and white gilded feathers at the bottom of my wings. "Umm, yeah. I told him."

"Scratch. Spit out whatever it is you're not saying," Evert says.

I shuffle my feet. "Hypothetically, if I said that these twelve cupid trainees in our den right now are really sucky cupids and that I need to train them for the next week, would you guys be understanding and supportive about the situation?"

Ronak and Evert sigh.

"Let me get this straight. Instead of quickly taking care of one last issue and then going on maternity leave, you invited a flock of cupids into our house and invited them to stay for a week," Ronak says dryly.

"Hypothetically," I answer.

He pinches the bridge of his nose and takes a deep breath.

"Get rid of them," Evert tells me.

"I hypothetically can't, because I hypothetically have to train them, or we'll be super behind, and I can't let Valentine's be ruined!" I argue.

"They can't stay in our den, Emelle," Sylred says calmly. "There isn't room."

"I know. Which is why I was hoping you'd be *understanding and supportive*, and help me figure out where to stash them when we aren't working. Hypothetically," I quickly add.

Based on the looks on their faces, I'm pretty sure my *hypothetically* isn't fooling anyone.

Sylred cocks his head in thought. "We can find a place for them."

"Don't encourage her. She was supposed to do one small thing, finish in an hour, and then be on leave," Ronak reminds him. "She was *not* supposed to agree to work for a week straight when she's about to have our baby any minute."

"Exactly," Evert adds, crossing his arms.

This is what happens when you mate with a bunch of dominating males. "Well, I *did* agree, so if you won't help me figure out where they can stay, I'll just do it myself!" I snap, turning to storm away. "Hypothetically!" I toss over my shoulder.

I don't even make it five steps before Okot intervenes. "My beloved," he says, gently taking hold of my arms.

I don't look up at him. I'm too mad.

"All of this arguing and stress is not good for you or the baby," he murmurs.

"Then tell *those genfins* to stop arguing with me," I retort.

Like a bad magic trick, all of *those genfins* step up so that I'm now surrounded by all four of my mates.

"I told you, of course we'll find a place for them to stay," Sylred says, moving my hair over my shoulder in a tender gesture.

Ronak wraps his tail around my waist, while Evert presses his chest against my back. Okot still has hold of my arms.

I narrow my eyes. "I know what you guys are doing, and it's not going to work."

Evert leans in and starts nipping at the back of my neck. "I don't know what you mean. Enlighten us."

"You're trying to soften me up with your sneak-touches."

"We aren't sneaking, little demon," Ronak says with a chuckle. "We upset you, and now we're comforting you."

"Why is Valentine's Day so important to you?" Sylred asks.

"Because. It's the one time of year where people actually seem to try. The dates. The thinking-of-you gifts. The flirting. The love. The sex. It's beautiful to see everyone taking a day to celebrate love. It's what we should do every day. Imagine what life would be like if everyone took the time to adore our loved ones—to express that love in whatever way is meaningful to them. As a cupid, that's the dream. That love would be cherished, always. So that's why Valentine's Day is important, okay? It reminds us to take a moment and appreciate our loved ones."

They all nod, like they get it, and they continue to rub on me. I frown and look down at all of their sweet touches, and my suspicion starts to build.

"Sorry for giving you a hard time, Scratch. We just want you to take a break and be able to relax," Evert says. "We understand the Valentine's thing."

Wait. Evert is *apologizing*? Okay, something is seriously up. He didn't even apologize for that time he left the toilet seat up, and I fell into the basin, getting gross toilet water all up in my business. I also got stuck. Yeah. *Stuck.* As in, I couldn't get my ass back out. I had to call for help, and Evert had to yank me out. Do you have any idea how humiliating that is? And the fucker laughed!

I narrow my eyes on him. "What's going on?"

"Nothing," Evert says too quickly.

I swing my eyes to Sylred. He can't keep anything from me. "Syl?"

He runs a hand through his pink hair a bit nervously. "Well, we received a message when we were walking back from town and—"

Evert slaps his hand over Sylred's mouth before he can say more. He then pulls out a letter from his pocket, but when I try to snatch it, he holds it over my head and hands it to Ronak.

I watch Ronak's brow furrow as his black eyes flit across the page. When he's done, he passes the letter back to Evert—who's still clamping a hand over Sylred's mouth. Sylred just stands there like he's glad he doesn't have to be the one to tell me what's going on.

"Well?" I ask, putting my hands on my hips.

Sylred and Evert both look to the alpha, and Ronak settles his gaze on me. "Our parents are back from vacation."

CHAPTER 8

I'm sitting on the floor of our shared closet in our bedroom, completely naked.

Crying. I'm also crying.

That's how Evert finds me.

He walks in, fresh out of the bath, and stops dead in his tracks. His blue eyes immediately go to my boobs. I mean, they're gigantic, so it's understandable. Still, it takes him a good five seconds to look up from them long enough to realize that I'm crying.

His eyes widen, and he immediately kneels down next to me. "What's wrong?"

"Nothing fits," I sniffle before digging into the food tin that's on my lap.

Evert grimaces. "How many times have we told you to stop eating fish right out of the can?"

Meeting his eye, I slowly lift the small fish and slurp it up like it's a spaghetti noodle.

"Fucking gross, Scratch."

"I'm hungry."

"It smells like rotten ass."

"I'm feeling attacked right now."

After eating the last of the fish, I tilt up the can and drink the juice out of it. Evert starts to gag.

He snatches the empty tin from me, storms out of the closet, and then stomps back in with a freshly warmed lime from the tree in our garden.

He tosses it to me, and I immediately peel it and start sucking on it like it's my favorite lollipop. I'm pretty sure he only gave it to me to help my fish breath, but I appreciate any time someone brings me food, regardless of the reason.

"Stop eating that fish shit, or I'm not gonna let you suck my cock anymore."

I snort. "As if."

He blinks down at me for a second and then shrugs. "Yeah, you're right. That was a bad bluff."

I crack the teensiest smile, which I know was his intent all along. He always knows how to make me laugh.

"Did you guys get all the cupids settled?"

He nods and sits down on the floor in front of me, taking my finished lime and chucking it behind him, not caring that it goes rolling on the floor in the bedroom. "We put them all up in town. Sev reminded them that if they fuck up and do any cupid shit while you're not around to supervise, he'll send them back to Cupidville and force them to do paperwork for ten years. That seemed to scare the little shits enough to behave for the night."

I nod and fidget with my hair.

"Scratch?"

I peer up at him through my lashes and sniffle. "Yeah?"

He presses his hand against my belly in a surprisingly gentle gesture and leans down so that we're eye-to-eye. Like the baby senses the attention, my belly stretches with a very obvious limb as the baby kicks and punches me. I frown as my skin stretches. "It looks like I have an alien trying to break out of me."

Evert just rubs everywhere the baby kicks. "He wants to come hang out with his dad."

I cock a brow. "He? You're so sure it's a boy?"

"It's definitely gonna be a boy this time," Evert says matter-of-factly.

I smile and rub my belly with him until the baby settles down. Kicking the hell out of me seems to really wear the poor thing out.

"So, you wanna tell me what's really bothering you, Scratch?"

I wipe my nose on my arm and shake my head. "Nothing. I'm good. Just another hormonal freak-out."

He gives me a look that says he's not buying it, and his black tail wraps around my arm. "If you're not up to going..."

"No, I want to go," I say quickly. He looks at my tear-streaked face dubiously. "I do. It's just, Resha..."

Evert shakes his head. "Ronak's mother is a bitch. Don't pay attention to her. The rest of our parents love you."

"Last time I saw Resha, I was five months pregnant with Amorette, and she told me that I was an unfit mate and that I must've tricked Ronak into bonding to me by using my 'creepy love magic,'" I remind him.

Evert frowns at the memory. "Yeah, and Ronak banned her after that. She hasn't been welcome here, but the letter made it sound like she's ready to swallow her fucking pride and get over herself."

"Yeah," I concede, still feeling conflicted.

"Just say the word, Scratch. If you don't want her there, we'll take care of it."

It's a sweet offer, and I know he means it, but I shake my head. "No, I want her there. I just want this to go better than the last time."

"Don't worry too much about it. Resha is a bitch. Always has been. You don't need to be worried about impressing her."

I snort a bit and then look down at my daunting belly. "Look at me. The only thing I could impress right now is a measuring tape, because I am freaking *wide*," I say, flopping my hands down my body.

"Hey, what are you doing in here?" I hear Sylred say as he, Ronak, and Okot all come walking in. Noticing my nude and puffy-eyed state, their expressions immediately turn concerned.

"What's wrong, my beloved?" Okot asks, kneeling down in front of me. He takes my feet and gently starts to massage the arches with his thumbs, giving just the right amount of pressure.

I moan in appreciation.

"Don't moan, or we'll all be walking out of here with hard dicks," Evert says.

"Can't help it. Feels good."

Okot smiles and continues to rub while Evert catches them up on why he found me naked and crying in the closet.

"If this is too stressful for you, tell us, and I'll cancel dinner," Ronak tells me.

I shake my head. "No. I want to go. I just want to prove

your mother wrong and show her that I am a good mate and a good mother," I tell him. "But I look like a puffer fish, and none of my dresses fit right," I admit, feeling self-conscious again.

"Then, it's fortunate that we brought someone here to help you with that," Ronak says with a playful smile.

CHAPTER 9

$\mathcal{I}$ look up at him curiously. "Someone to help me? Who?" I ask curiously.

Instead of answering me, Sylred passes me a robe, and Evert moves so that I can slip it on. Okot helps me to stand, and then they lead me to the front of the room where my friend Mossie is playing on the floor with my daughter.

I smile when I see her showing Amorette how to properly water her scalp where her vines and flowers grow.

Spotting me, Mossie stands and claps. "There you are! Just wait to see all the dresses your mates had me pick up. You're going to look so pretty!"

The guys stay in the front room with Amorette while Mossie and I wander back into my bedroom. I hadn't noticed before, but there's a heap of dresses already lying on the bed, along with a row of new silk slippers.

"Okay," Mossie says, wasting no time. "Let's get you prettied up to meet the parents so they can love you as much as I do."

51

I strip off my robe as she starts tugging on my first dress choice. "What if they don't?" I ask nervously.

Her bright green eyes narrow on the white dress, and she immediately yanks it off of me and goes through the pile to select another one. "If they don't, then screw them. You're *the* cupid. You single-handedly killed our tyrannical prince with a Love Arrow through the heart. You helped set the realm back to the way it should be, where all fae are considered equal. Because of you, there are no more culling games or prison towers full of innocents. We actually got to have a say in who became our new monarch, and the new king and queen are the best we've had in centuries, because of *you*. You're an awesome mother, and based on how much your guys are always getting stiff sticks in public, you're a great mate, too. You are amazing," she says, yanking on the ties at my back as she fits me into another dress.

"Thanks, Moss," I say quietly. "Hey, how are things with...what was his name? Turny?"

"Oh, him," she says dismissively. "I ended things."

"Another one? That's like, the fourth dump this month."

She shrugs. "He wasn't meeting my needs. Or the needs of my flowers," she says, running a hand over the sunflowers popping out of her head.

I'm pretty sure I don't want her to go into detail about that, so I let it drop.

Mossie walks around me, looking me up and down, her lips puckered together in thought. Finally, she shakes her head. "Yellow is not your color," she says decisively before yanking it off me.

She sorts through a few more options, muttering to herself about bodice styles, colors, and other crap, until she finally picks up a silvery dress. She pulls it over my head, and I immediately like the fabric. It's soft and smooth and doesn't feel heavy like the other options.

When Mossie finishes doing up the ties in the back, she comes around the front to inspect me, and a smile spreads across her green-tinged face. "This is the one."

"Are you sure?" I ask, running my hands nervously down the front.

I move to walk over to the full-length mirror, but she stops me by clamping a hand over my eyes. "Nope. No looking until I've done your hair and makeup. Now come on, I've got everything already set up in the bathroom."

She tugs me out of the bedroom and into the bathroom, and I sit down at the vanity, facing away from the mirror.

Mossie sets to work with my hair first, combing it with precision as she winds parts of my pink hair to look like I have a band of roses stretching across the top. She adds crystals into the center and then smooths the rest of my frizzy waves with a lightly-scented oil, curling whatever wayward strands she finds with a small brass cylinder.

When she's satisfied with that, she starts dusting my face with all types of powders, liners, and color stains.

She even comes at me with scissors and weird copper things that look like some form of medieval tweezers. She starts plucking away at my eyebrows, making me flinch back in surprise.

"Ouch!" I say with a frown.

She doesn't stop or slow down, though, and starts plucking at me like a chicken. When she yanks out a particularly painful patch, I clamp my hand over my poor eyebrows and smack her hand away. "Okay! Enough! I can't handle it."

"Please. You pushed Amorette out of your vagina. Your *vagina*," she stresses, as if I somehow forgot my sixteen-hour labor, where all I had for pain relief was some poppleberries and a shot of pixie juice. Pain relief, my ass. I felt *everything*.

"You can handle this," she assures me right after smacking my hand away from my forehead and continuing to pluck. "Luckily, you have a lovely natural arch. But it's all about the cleanup. You've got to keep up on these things. Don't think I didn't notice your chickweeds. I'll be stopping by to wax those for you."

I immediately cover my crotch area with my hands. "You come anywhere near my vagina right now, and I will make you fall in love with that guy who liked to snack on his mother's fingernail clippings."

She wrinkles her nose in disgust. "Are threats really necessary?"

"When you want to pour hot wax on my girl grotto, then yes, threats are appropriate."

She rolls her eyes and sets down the tweezers finally before putting some finishing touches on my eyes and lips. "There," she says proudly. "All done. You're gonna dazzle them."

She helps me stand, and I turn around to face the mirror. My jaw opens in surprise. I don't even recognize my reflection. Instead of the slouchy hot mess I've been lately, I look like more than just a fat pregnant chick who can't see her feet.

The dress accentuates my curves without making me look bigger. The material hugs my body without it being tight, making it look like I'm not just a big ball of blob.

The top of it dips down just barely between my breasts, highlighting my boobs while still somehow being somewhat modest. It ends in a train of soft silvery shimmers that drags behind me, and the sleeves flare out at my wrists.

My pink hair is perfectly coiffed, and the rose twirls she's created make me look like some kind of flower princess. My makeup isn't too heavy, only being bold at the eyes where she's lined them in black and added a subtle dusting of shimmer to the lids.

"Mossie, you made me look beautiful," I say in surprise.

She rolls her eyes. "You're *always* beautiful, I just helped polish you up a bit. You look like the best covey mate there's ever been. Own it."

When I start to tear up, she reaches up and smacks me on my cheeks. I flinch back, startled, and we blink at each other. "Sorry, I panicked," she admits. "I didn't want you to mess up the eye makeup I worked so hard on. No crying."

I'm too afraid of getting slapped again, so I nod. "Okay. Noted."

"Sorry, my lady garden has been growing thorns all week. I've been a bit on edge."

I wince on her behalf. "That sounds awful."

"It is," she says seriously. She grabs my arm and starts leading me out of the bathroom. "Come on, let's go make your mates drool. I'm watching Amorette tonight for you."

"Thanks, Moss. She always loves staying with you."

"That's because she has excellent taste," Mossie replies primly.

Reaching the end of the hallway, Mossie stops me and

walks in first. I hear her clap. "Okay, cupid mates, pay attention! Your female is ready to make her debut."

Feeling jittery with nerves, I walk out, and all four of my mates stand up and turn around to face me.

Four sets of eyes lock onto me, and the air charges with intensity.

"And that's our cue. Come on, kid." Mossie picks up Amorette and walks over.

"You look pretty, Mommy."

I smile and kiss her. "Thank you, baby. Be good for Mossie, okay?"

Amorette nods excitedly. "I will. She's gonna let me plant new seeds on her head."

"Oh. That's nice."

"See you later," Mossie says, giving me an air kiss. "Don't eat too much and then pass out snoring on the restaurant's floor."

"That was one time," I frown.

She shrugs. "People still talk about it."

No regrets.

$\mathcal{M}$ ossie disappears out the door with Amorette in tow, and I face my mates, absentmindedly wringing my hands. I look at each of them, and they're all staying stubbornly silent.

After a few more seconds, I can't stand it anymore. "Well? Do I look okay?" I ask anxiously.

When I see Evert shake his head, my nerves spike. "No. You don't look okay. You look fucking gorgeous."

I swallow thickly at the heated look in his eye.

"He speaks the truth," Okot agrees in his magnanimous way of speaking. "You are a vision, my beloved."

Sylred steps forward and gently cups my cheek, pressing his lips to the corner of my mouth. "You're perfect. As always."

When he steps back, I notice that my guys are all dressed to impress as well, wearing very debonair clothing. They're all in black or white, impeccably fitted tunics and pants, held up by fancy belts. Ronak has shaved his brown head of hair short and trimmed his beard, while Sylred has his pink hair combed, the longer ends curling at the base of his skull and behind his ears. Evert's black hair is tousled but neat, and even though he shaved, his pale skin always shows the sexy shadow across his jaw that I love. Okot's bright red mohawk is slicked back, and they all look so freaking handsome I'm tempted to push the nearest one down and ride him right here on the floor.

"She's giving us sex eyes again," Evert muses, his lips curling up mischievously.

"Can you blame me? You guys look hot. If we're quick, can we just…"

They chuckle, and Sylred shakes his head. "Not if we want to be on time."

I try to hide the disappointment on my face, but I don't think it works, because Evert laughs again. "I'm with Scratch. Let's blow off the fuckers and stay here. I'd much rather peel off that dress she's wearing and have our wicked way with her than go to dinner, anyway."

"Don't encourage her," Sylred laughs. "We'll peel off her dress later," he adds, shooting me a wink.

"I'm going to hold you to that," I warn him.

"Oh, we'll give you something to hold," Evert adds, wagging his eyebrows.

Ronak comes forward and holds his elbow out to me. "May I escort you?" he asks, surprising me with the gentleness to his voice.

"You may," I say, shyly taking his arm.

He leads me up the stairs and outside. The soft, lavender light of dusk shrouds the landscape, and I can hear birds singing the last of their songs as we make our way to the end of the path.

Waiting on the road is an extra-large wooden carriage that is roomy enough to comfortably fit all five of us.

Ronak helps me inside, and I settle between him and Sylred while Okot and Evert sit across from us.

The carriage driver urges the horses forward, and I start mentally going over all seven of their parents' names. I know that they've all lost at least one father, but Sylred lost his mother, too. Sylred has two fathers still alive: Yored and Perel. Evert has his mother, Evia, and his father, Welk. Ronak has his two fathers, Hesh and Gullen. And then of course, Ronak's mother, Resha.

I say the names over and over again in my head, but I'm probably making a weird face, because Evert cocks a brow. "Thinking too hard again?"

I nod. "Yeah," I say honestly. "Your family has a lot of names, and since we don't see them much, I'm doing flash cards."

Evert's eyes flick down to my empty hands and then back to meet my gaze. "Mental flashcards. Like, in my head," I explain.

A grin spreads across his face. "Of course."

"I have a plan," I say after a few more minutes of name-flashing.

"Oh, yeah? And what's the plan?" Sylred asks.

"I decided I'm just gonna make Ronak's mother like me."

The guys blink at me.

"I have it all planned out. She's probably still a bit mad that I'm not a nice, high-society genfin female like Delsheen, and she's also probably upset about the fact that we haven't let her come see us or be around Amorette. So, to deflect away from all of that negativity, I'm just going to be so lovable that it'll be impossible not to like me, and then all of that disapproval will be water under the bridge. See? Easy," I tell them, looking around expectantly.

They're bound to realize my geniusness and comment on it.

Silence follows.

Yep, they'll probably commend me any second now...

Still nothing.

I frown. "It's a good idea," I tell them, because clearly, they haven't deduced this on their own. I guess we can't all be geniuses in this covey. Good thing they're so hot.

"Just so that I'm understanding this right, your plan is to force Resha to like you?" Evert asks.

"Exactly." I smile.

Ronak clears his throat. "My mother is very alpha. She has always run the household and my fathers since I was a child. She has very strong opinions, and she doesn't hold back, even when she should. Honestly, I'm not expecting much from her tonight."

"What he means is his mom is a bitch and everyone knows it," Evert says dryly.

Ronak doesn't even get mad at that. He just shrugs.

"Yeah, well, I'm totally gonna cure her bitchiness. After tonight, I'm going to be her new favorite person. Just watch."

Evert chuckles. "This oughta be good."

The carriage lurches to a stop, and I peek out the window, seeing that we've arrived at the fancy restaurant in town. The street is busy with some kind of fair, so vendors and entertainers are out in droves, and the entire road is lit up by lanterns and magical twinkle lights hanging from every building.

"Ready?" Sylred asks, offering his hand.

"Yep, totally ready."

CHAPTER 11

The restaurant is a super fancy genfin establishment, and the place is packed. The building, like all the others, is dome-shaped and made out of polished wood. When we walk in, the lighting is low, and I can see into an exclusive bar area in the back, while there's a set of spiral stairs that go underground to the restaurant below. Like the outside, everything is made of smooth, polished wood.

As we approach, a genfin host comes forward. "Covey Fircrown," he greets us. "Right this way. The rest of your party is already waiting."

The host leads us to the spiral stairs, and like everything else, they're wooden, polished, and while very nice craftsmanship, they're narrow and steep. I take a deep, fortifying breath to prepare myself for this formidable journey.

"Okay, Emelle. You can do this," I say, cricking my neck side to side to really amp myself up.

The host and my other mates turn around and look at me expectantly.

"Are you giving yourself a pep talk?" Evert chuckles beside me.

"Do you see those stairs? It's like a deathtrap."

"We would never let you fall, my beloved," Okot reassures me.

I walk forward, and the host begins his descent down the death stairs. Ronak keeps his steady gaze on me. "I'll go in front, and you can hold on to me," he says. Then he turns his head to Okot. "You walk behind her," the alpha orders.

Okot nods, and then Ronak turns and heads for the stairs. He doesn't start descending until my hand grabs his forearm that he's holding against his back just for me. You wouldn't think walking down stairs would be such a big thing, but since *I'm* a big thing, it is.

With one hand on his arm and one hand on the railing, I carefully start to make my way down, but it's dark and daunting as hell since I can't see my feet or even the steps. I feel pretty badass, to be honest. Every stair that I manage to make it down is like winning a championship.

I'm nearly at the last step when my foot misses the stair completely, and I start to freefall. I barely get a little shriek out before I feel Okot pluck me up effortlessly, his hands under my arms.

I look over my shoulder. "Oh my gods. My life just flashed before my eyes."

Okot smiles and sets me down at the bottom of the steps.

"I totally rocked those stairs," I say.

"You tripped," Evert deadpans.

"Yeah, but not until the end," I argue.

He just chuckles.

I step up beside Ronak, whose arm is crooked and waiting for me.

"You okay?" Ronak checks.

"Yeah, it was just a little fall. Like, a tenth of a fall. I knew it was gonna happen, so I was already mentally prepared. Just like I knew I was gonna fall off that obstacle course you made me train on after Amorette was born. Remember? I nearly died."

Ronak rolls his eyes. "You were three feet in the air, and there was a safety net under you."

"Yeah, but those three feet were terrifying."

"I caught you," he reminds me.

"Specifics aren't necessary for this story." I wave my hand dismissively.

I grab his arm and look around at all the dark, round wooden tables and plush sofa-like chairs. The space is lit up by candles and twinkling fairy lights, and nearly every table is full with genfins dressed in fancy clothes.

When the dessert tray rolls by, I start salivating so much that I kind of choke on my spit. Evert pats me on the back unhelpfully.

"Right this way, Covey Fircrown," the host says, leading us through the room.

Everyone we pass looks up from their meal to stare at us. My covey and I are kind of famous since we took down the prince. Since Ronak and I have matching cupid wings, Sylred and I have matching pink hair, and I have a huge lamassu mate, we kind of stick out. Evert is the only one who can somewhat fade into the background, but he doesn't anyway, because he's Evert. Which means he's usually cursing louder than what's appropriate for polite society.

Ronak strides forward effortlessly, his chin up, looking

fine as hell. I try to do my best to glide next to him, but there's just no gliding in my current form. When we near a large table near the back, my eyes fall on a group of seven older genfins.

They all stand as we approach the table, except for one. Ronak's mother, Resha, stays sitting down at one end of the long table. This doesn't bode well for a fresh start.

She has dark gray hair swept up on her head, familiar black eyes that match Ronak's, and a formidable expression. Stopping before them, our eyes lock, and I watch as she takes me in from my toes to the top of my head. Her eyes linger on my cupid wings, shifting from mine to the pair on Ronak's back. She sniffs and raises her nose in the air. I plaster a smile on my face.

"Hello, Resha. How are you?" I step forward and go in for a hug. Except I have a hard time bending down right now on account of being middle-heavy. So I kind of fall on top of her where she sits in her chair. My smiling face smooshes against her cheek, and I get a little spit on her. "Whoopsies!" I laugh nervously, trying to pick myself back up. I can't. I've totally lost my balance. Ronak comes to my rescue and pulls me back so that I can stand again.

"Whew! Sorry." I smile down at her. She just glares at me and swipes a hand across her cheek where my slobber and some of my makeup rubbed onto her.

"Mother," Ronak nods at her.

"Son."

They do some intense eye lock, where neither of them backs down. It gets tense, so I quickly intervene. "So, Resha. I love what you've done with your hair."

Resha sniffs and lifts her glass of water. "I haven't done anything to my hair."

My smile starts to waver, but I keep that sucker locked

in place, because I'm on a mission, dammit. "Well, it still looks super awesome."

She gives my pink hair a long look, letting me know that she doesn't trust my judgment.

Ronak's fathers, Hesh and Gullen, come forward and shake my hand. They look similar with gray hair and brown eyes. All three of Ronak's parents have brown tails and wings that have gone slightly silver with age. I haven't seen them since the last mishap with Resha, because Ronak banned them too.

Evia is already hugging Evert and trying to straighten his clothes. She always dotes on him. She's a short little thing, only coming up to his sternum, and while her face is lined with wrinkles, she has a pair of dimples that she obviously passed down to her son. "Look at you! Not eating enough. You're practically skin and bones," she says, pinching him on the stomach.

He flinches slightly and rolls his eyes. "It's called training. I'm not a flabby son of a bitch like father," Evert jokes, laughing at the male who comes up to clap him on the back.

The male, Welk, pats his sizable stomach. "What, this? This is pure muscle."

Evert laughs and shakes his head. "Sure it is."

Behind me, Sylred is greeting his fathers as well, Yored and Perel, and I can tell by their shy and quiet demeanors that that's where Sylred got his level-headed peacekeeping ways from. The parents have all been travelling together, so we haven't seen them in months.

Evert's mother comes up to me next. I start to hold out my hand in greeting, but she just throws herself forward and wraps me in a hug.

"Fucking hell, Ma. Go easy on my mate," Evert chastises.

Evia is a good head shorter than me, and her arms can't reach all the way around my middle, but she doesn't seem to mind because she just starts to rub my belly like it's a genie's lamp.

"Look at the home you've grown for my grandbaby!" Evia says excitedly to my belly. "I haven't seen you in ages!" She looks me up and down and nods approvingly. "I've told you before, you've got good hips, Emelle. That's important, you know. Good hips can make all the difference in labor. How are you feeling? Any lightning crotch?"

I blink at her. "Ummm…"

"Ma, don't get fucking weird and talk about my mate's crotch," Evert cuts in.

Evia rounds on him, putting her hands on her hips in a very motherly fashion. "Evert, I really wish you wouldn't swear."

He just leans in and pecks her on the cheek. She melts instantly, and her scowl turns to a beaming smile. She smacks him on the arm. "Oh, I just can't stay mad at you!"

"Let's sit," Ronak says, leading me to the table.

I move to the left, so that Ronak can sit at the other head, directly across from his mother, but he stops me. In a deliberate move, he sits *me* down at the head of the table, so now it's me and Resha facing off.

When Resha narrows her eyes at me, I make a face at Ronak, but he just sits down on the chair to my right and places a hand on my thigh. I don't know if it's to offer comfort or to make sure I don't bolt.

He's really messing up my *Operation: Make Resha Love Me* mission.

CHAPTER 12

*W*hen we're all sitting, the table soon picks up with several conversations at once, and I watch as my genfins reconnect with their parents. Okot sits on my left and joins in the talks. It admittedly took a bit for them to get used to having another non-genfin in our covey, but the males saw him turn into his lamassu bull form once, and they've respected him ever since.

By the time the food arrives, the guys and their parents have shed the stuffiness of their first meeting, and now they're all swapping stories about their time apart. The guys and I catch them up on all things Amorette, which is always a sure way to get everyone on the same page. Except Ronak's parents, of course. Since Ronak banned them, they haven't actually met Amorette yet. I'm hoping to fix that.

Huge platters of tender meat, grilled vegetables, and spiced rice get brought out, and each of the alphas from each covey serves his mate first before serving the rest of his covey. It's such a sweet gesture to see Ronak serving me, Okot, Evert, and Sylred, and I can't help the smile that spreads across my face.

"How was your vacation?" I ask Resha. I have to kind of yell since we're sitting at opposite ends of the table, so everyone else's conversations cut off as they wait to see what she'll say.

Resha takes a bite of her food and chews extra slowly, making me wait. I just keep smiling patiently. Finally, she says, "It was fine."

My eye twitches a bit. She sure isn't making this easy on me. "The guys tell me that you all went to visit one of the tropical islands south of here. That must have been lovely."

"There were too many insects."

I start scratching my arm. "Oh, that's too bad. You guys do have crazy-looking bugs. There were some gross ones on the Earth realm, but those are nothing compared to the bugs here. I found a bug in my closet a few weeks ago that looked like a giant grasshopper except with people-lips." I pucker up my lips and tap them to demonstrate. "They were seriously luscious. I was tempted to grab some lipstick and put it on the thing. But I'm pretty sure it catcalled to me when I walked by, so I threw a bowl over it and waited for Ronak to come home so he could take it outside."

Resha looks like I'm going to make her ears bleed if I don't stop talking. "If you were a proper genfin mate, you would not cower in your own home because of a little bug," she says.

"This sucker wasn't small."

She just stares at me, unimpressed.

I look over at Ronak a bit desperately. "It was as big as Ronak's—"

He clamps a hand over my mouth before I can finish. The parents shift uncomfortably in their chairs. Evert snickers.

"Mother," Ronak says, addressing her. "Stop being so difficult to Emelle."

She just sniffs and raises her chin haughtily.

I try to push Ronak's hand off my mouth, but he doesn't let go. I stick my tongue out and slather it all over his palm, but that doesn't work either, so I change tactics and push his fingers even further in, and then I bite him. Hard.

He snatches his hand away, and I rush to explain. "I was gonna say the bug was as big as Ronak's foot!" I say primly. I turn to glare at Ronak for making it seem worse than it was. "I wasn't gonna say it was as big as your co—"

He clamps a hand over my mouth again.

That time it was justified. Whoops.

Ronak's fathers look like they want to crawl into a genfin cave and hide.

Ronak leans in to speak into my ear. "Can you not talk about the size of my dick at the dinner table with our parents?"

I nod and a muffled *yep* comes out against his hand.

He drops his hand again, and I smile sheepishly. "Words just come out sometimes," I tell his parents.

"That kind of thing would never happen to a nice high-ranking society girl like that Delsheen," Resha says.

The fork in my hand nearly bends from me clutching it so hard.

Don't forking stab her, don't forking stab her, don't forking stab her.

I smile tightly. "Delsheen is a self-absorbed jerk."

Resha smooths her gray hair. "Yes, but she has excellent table manners."

"I totally have good table manners," I blurt out.

Resha cocks a thin brow and looks down at my plate. Okay, plates. Plural. I have four. And yeah, I ate most of it with my fingers, so my cloth napkin is covered in meat stains, and not the sexual kind.

I quickly pile my four plates up on top of each other, but there's still food on some of them, so it kind of makes this weird unsteady tower. "There," I say proudly. "Oh, wait." I take the gross napkin and smooth it out before folding it into a fancy heart shape. I place it on top of the plate tower. "That's better," I say proudly.

"Hmm," Resha says.

Operation Love Me isn't going so well.

"Mother, just because Emelle is being so kind and forgiving about your behavior tonight, doesn't mean that I am. If you want to meet your granddaughter, then I expect you to treat her with respect, and I don't ever want to hear you bring up Delsheen's name again, is that clear?" Ronak says as his tail curls around my calf.

"Delsheen was a nightmare," Evia cuts in. "I'm glad you didn't mate to her."

The other fathers nod. "Yes, she was quite difficult," Sylred's father adds.

"She comes from good genfin blood," Resha argues.

"She fucked the prince during our mating celebration," Evert says dryly.

"Evert! Don't swear at the dinner table," Evia scolds.

He just shrugs.

"I apologize for my mother's behavior," Ronak says to me, although he does it loudly enough that it's clear he wants his mother to hear. "Let's go."

70

"Wait," I blurt. "Why don't we all go enjoy the fair? It'll be fun!"

Evert's parents are already nodding, Sylred's fathers look a bit nervous, and Ronak's fathers are watching Resha for confirmation either way.

If I'm going to get her to love me, then I can't just let the night end like this. Ronak is pissed, which means he'll probably ban her again, and then I'll have to wait another long stint before I get to try again. I want Amorette to be able to spend time with all of her grandparents, and I want Ronak to have a relationship with his parents again. I love Ronak for always putting me first. I love that my alpha adores me enough to cut his parents off for disrespecting me. It proves just how much he's in my corner. But I know he misses his family, so I'm determined to change things.

"It will be great," I say, my high-beam smile on. "I bet there'll be honey cakes. Will there be honey cakes?" I ask.

"I'm sure we can find you some," Sylred assures me.

"I could do with some honey cakes," Evert's father says.

I smile at him. "Exactly! Honey cakes are the best."

Sylred's father Perel says, "I prefer chocolate."

I start gagging.

Yep. Just the mention of chocolate these days sends me into a fit of heaves. It's heartbreaking. Sylred had to throw away all of his old pants since he couldn't get the chocolate scent out of his pockets.

Okot rubs my back while my eyes water, and I try to convince my stomach to keep everything down.

"Was it something I said?" I hear Perel ask.

"She can't tolerate the *C* word," Okot says politely.

Evert snickers again.

By the time I manage to stop gagging, I'm pretty sure

my eye makeup is ruined because I have tears running down my cheeks. I pick up my soiled heart napkin and start dabbing myself. I'm pretty sure all I'm doing is just smearing meat juice on my face, though. Again, not the sex kind.

CHAPTER 13

Okot takes the gross, juicy napkin from me, and replaces it with his super clean one and uses it to dab my face. When he's done, he leans back, his red-ringed eyes roaming over my face adoringly. "There, my beloved."

Gods, this guy. I lean forward and press a kiss to his lips, wishing I could run my hands through his mohawk and have my way with him. "Thank you, Okot."

"There she goes, using her love magic on them," I hear Resha grumble.

I look up, surprised. "I didn't use love magic."

"I'm sure that's how you got them to mate with you in the first place," Resha says haughtily.

"Nope. It was her tits," Evert deadpans.

His dad chuckles, his mother hisses his name, and Sylred smacks him on the back of his head.

"I've never used love magic on any of your sons," I announce. Then, thinking about that, I say, "Well, okay, I Lusted them a bunch of times, but mostly because it was funny, and—"

"See! She admits it!" Resha exclaims, now deigning to stand like the rest of us. "She tricked our sons into mating with her!"

I frown. "That's not—"

The restaurant host comes over to ask us to be quiet, but one snarl from Ronak, and the male goes scurrying away.

"Not like that," I argue. "I never would've forced them to love me. That's not how it works, anyway. My Love Arrows wouldn't work unless there were already some inclination there, and—"

"You don't have to explain yourself," Ronak cuts me off angrily. I know his anger is directed at his mother and not me, but I still hate the direction this dinner has taken.

"I want to," I insist, wringing my hands. This has turned into a giant ball of shitcluster. "I'm barely even a cupid these days, to be honest. I hardly ever use my power. I'm lazy. Plus, I'm pretty sure I have some cupid PTSD from all the lonely years I was stuck on the Earth realm working. But...yeah, lazy. It's mostly because I'm lazy," I admit. "The cupid thing? Psh. Barely do it."

Of course, that's when a dozen cupids come filing down the stairs.

Shitty heartsharts. Why do I always have the worst timing?

Resha glares at me. "I think it's fair to say that I can add dishonesty to your list of attributes."

"Did I say barely? I meant that I do impromptu cupid training once in a while," I quickly amend.

Sev notices me and saunters up, the trainees following behind him like little ducklings. "Hey there, boss. Fancy place, aye?"

"What are you doing here?" I hiss.

"Cupid shitheads gotta eat, get it? This place looked the fanciest. Told the prickler upstairs to put us on your tab, since you're the fooking boss and all," he says with a grin. "Figured, if you're gonna teach 'em how to shoot their fooking arrows, you can feed 'em, too."

I swear, there's no way I have proper karma or lady luck magic, because this shit would not happen to me if those powers were working correctly.

"Sev, go find a table and make sure you and all of the cupids behave yourselves."

Sev buries his hands in his pockets. He's wearing super tight leather pants, too, so it's a feat. "I was thinkin' I'd start a bit of an orgy in this place. Call it homework."

My eyes widen. "Don't you even *think* about it."

He laughs. "Relax, boss. I'm only yankin' ya."

"Don't yank my mate," Evert snaps.

I clap my hands to disrupt them before Sev can spout off something else that will piss Evert off. "Okay! This is fun. Let's all go to the fair. I'm ready, who's ready?"

I start hefting myself up out of the seat, but Ronak takes over and lifts me with one arm. This time, he doesn't even let me try to walk the stairs by myself. He just scoops me up and carries me up and doesn't set me down until we're out of the restaurant and on the street.

I catch a whiff of something that smells sugary and delicious, and see that now that night has fallen, the street fair is in full swing. There's music echoing around us, lanterns, genfins buying trinkets and watching street performers, and more delicious food smells that keep wafting toward me.

"I love street fairs!" I beam.

"The last time you went to one, you drank too much fairy wine, and you tried to do something called twerking on the knife thrower's stage. You tripped, and when the knife thrower tried to catch you, he ended up with a blade in his neck for his troubles," Sylred reminds me, his brown eyes sparkling with humor.

"The stage was slippery," I defend.

Evert snorts. "That's because you grabbed a full bottle of wine and dumped it on the stage, claiming you were 'marinating the wood.'"

Yeah. I did it.

"Maybe the fair isn't such a good idea..." Sylred's father says, looking worried.

"Oh, don't worry. No wine for me until after the baby is born. Let's go!"

I start leading the way, and to my surprise, all of the parents follow, even Ronak's. It's the longest I've been around Resha to date. I hang back and loop my arm through hers. She tenses at the touch but doesn't immediately fling me off, so I take that as a win.

Ronak looks at me like I'm crazy, but I just wave him off. My other mates start talking with their parents, and pretty soon, we're right in the thick of the fair, surrounded by genfins.

Lined up and down the street are food carts, trinkets for sale, dancing, acrobatics and flight shows, fortune tellers, and some genfins putting on a magic fire show.

"So. Resha. How many years have you been mated?" I ask, going for friendly conversation.

"One hundred and seventy-three years," she answers.

"Wow. That's a super long time. How's that going?"

"My covey is honorable, and all of my mates have high ranking genfin blood. My parents arranged us, and it was the perfect match."

My mouth drops open, and I yank her to a stop. "Oh

my gods. That's why you're so grumpy. You guys don't love each other!"

She scowls at me and disentangles my hold from her arm. "Do not start spouting off things that you know nothing about."

I'm kicking myself right now for not realizing this sooner. Now that I'm mindful, I open up my cupid senses, and immediately, I can feel the shift. Resha is totally thirsty for some lovin'.

"Don't you worry, MIL. I got you. I just need to round up my cupids and grab a few Love Arrows," I explain. "We'll get this sorted right away."

Resha's face scrunches up real tight until she looks about ready to explode, but instead of yelling at me, she just spins on her heels and marches away.

"Okay! We'll do it later, then!"

She ignores me.

"What was that about?" Okot asks, coming up beside me.

"I totally figured out how to get Resha to love me," I say smugly.

Okot looks at me curiously, but before I can explain, I get distracted by a stand selling glass dildos. I must say it out loud, because Evert is suddenly at my side laughing. "Those aren't dildos, Scratch. Those are rolling pins."

I squint around people to get a better look. "Oh. You're right. That's boring." I cock my head in thought. "I bet you could use it as a dildo, though."

"For the last time, you don't need any dildos. You have four fucking mates."

"Yeah, but these ones have glitter, and they come in different colors. Ooh! And that one has magic fire inside of it!"

Evert quickly steers me away. We come up to a game tent next, and Ronak wins a handmade doll to give to Amorette. Next, we hit the fortune teller, the fire show, the flying genfin acrobatics, and of course, the honey stand. No one gets chocolate.

Okot buys me a crown of flowers to wear, and Sylred dances with me on the dance floor while the fae band plays music. My feet are killing me, and I'm so tired I'm pretty sure I can fall asleep standing up, but one of the elders intercepts us as we're on our way back to the carriage.

He's balding, with one last patch of hair hanging on for dear life at the top of his head.

"Elder Mortel," Ronak says with a respectful nod. "How can we help you?"

He turns to me. "Emelle, there are cupids in my restaurant," he says, sounding unhappy.

Cupid crapcakes. I think I'm in trouble.

CHAPTER 14

I go for innocence, and I twirl my hair around my finger. If he is mad about me bringing cupids here, maybe I can distract him long enough to waddle away.

I blurt out the first thing that comes to mind. "Oh, do you own that restaurant, Elder Mortel? It's super nice. The stairs were kinda scary. The lighting was good, though. And the meat. The meat was extra juicy."

I don't know what it is with me and meat juice tonight.

"Was I supposed to get, like, a cupid permit? A realm visa? I'm not sure how this works, but I'm sorry if I was supposed to get your permission first."

Elder Mortel cuts me off. "I actually have a request for you."

I blink in surprise. "Oh. Okay."

"There are three mating ceremonies taking place in two days. Unfortunately, we've run out of our genfin mating nectar. You remember?" he asks. "The chalice you drank out of with the blood added?"

My cheeks instantly warm at the memory of my

genfins and me in heat. It was…intense. But…wait. "What exactly *is* genfin nectar?"

Sylred cringes. "You don't want to know."

Okay. Moving on.

"Without that nectar, genfins don't go into heat. And without going into heat, their bond won't properly form, and if the bond doesn't form, then their covey magic doesn't connect."

I'm pretty sure he's asking me to make a bunch of genfins horny for each other.

"Please," he says when I don't answer right away. "Our resources are low, and the nectar won't be ready for another month."

"Of course I'll help," I say, putting him at ease. "This is actually perfect. I'll bring my trainees with me, and they can do it as their assignment. It'll be excellent practice before Valentine's Day."

He has no idea what Valentine's means, but he rolls with it and gives me a smile. "Perfect! The ceremonies will take place in the pavilion at nightfall. I can trust you and your cupids to be there?"

"Totally."

The elder pats me on the shoulder and mutters something about *helpful cupids* before walking off.

I instantly turn to my mates with a beaming smile. "Did you see that? Your genfin elder totally just asked *me* for help."

"We saw," Sylred chuckles.

"That was so awesome! And now I'll get to give my cupids some real-life experience."

"Was that…Elder Mortel?"

I turn to look at Resha as she comes pushing through the other parents.

80

I nod. "Yep."

"He's the most prominent member on the elder council. Why was he talking to you?"

"He asked me for help," I say proudly.

She frowns.

"Ready to go?" Ronak asks me.

I nod as a yawn overtakes me. "Yep. Someone carry me, though. I'm too tired to walk. Also, my feet hurt. Also, I want another honey cake for the road."

"Already got it for you," Sylred says, handing me one.

"Gods, you're just the best," I say, taking it.

We say our goodbyes to the parents, and then I look between Ronak and Okot as I bite into the cake, waiting to see who will take me. Ronak rolls his eyes, but he scoops me up bridal style and starts heading away.

When we're back in the carriage, I rest my head against Sylred's shoulder. "That was fun."

Sylred kisses the top of my head. "It was."

"Resha totally almost likes me," I say around a yawn.

"You have nothing to prove to my mother," Ronak says with a frown.

"Yeah. She's a bitch. She calls her housekeeper, Housekeeper. The male has worked for her for fifty years, and she still can't call the fucker by name. Don't kill yourself trying to impress her," Evert says.

"I think she's just unhappy," I admit. "I realized that I don't pick up any love mojo coming off of her."

I peek up at Ronak to see how he receives this news, but he just looks resigned.

"You know that your parents aren't in love?" I ask, surprised.

Ronak just shrugs. "Most genfin mate matches are arranged. The males put in a request for a mate, but it has to be approved by the elders. Since there are so few genfin females, it's usually multiple coveys vying for the same female. The one with the highest social standing gets first choice."

"Huh. That's sad."

"It's just the way things are."

"Love isn't guaranteed just because people bond as mates. We got lucky," Sylred says.

My eye twitches with power, and a pile of four-leaf clovers lands on our laps out of nowhere.

We stare in surprise for a beat, and then my guys just simply dust themselves off, shoving the clovers to the floor. They're used to my weird magical bouts by now. Nothing really fazes them much.

I spend the rest of the carriage ride mulling over the conversation. Now it all makes sense. Why Viessa, another genfin female, asked me to help her to love her mates. Why Ronak's mother doesn't seem happy. How genfin mate matches are made. It's sad to me knowing that most of them don't even love the genfins that they're bonded to.

Coming up with an idea, I smile to myself.

Evert narrows his eyes at me. "What's that for?"

"I'm just smiling. I like to smile," I defend.

"You're planning something."

The other guys groan. Even Okot.

I get a lot of that. Granted, some of my ideas are not the best. Like the time I planned to surprise Sylred by carving him a new instrument. I nearly lost a finger. Not mine—Evert's. He still has a scar.

Oh, well. This time, my idea is brilliant, and there's almost zero chance of me cutting off anyone's body parts. At least, I hope.

CHAPTER 15

"*A*gain!"

I get a chorus of groans in response.

I frown at the cupid trainees lined up. The girl with the cell phone is sitting down in the grass, muttering about how she wants to update her status, then insists that shooting arrows is not ladylike. The goth dudes are hanging out together smoking a pipe that I'm pretty sure they swiped from my house, and the nerdy guy with the lisp and buckteeth keeps picking his nose and eating it when he thinks no one is watching.

"Come on, cupids, try again!"

I'm surprised when they suddenly jolt to do my bidding. Huh. Maybe they're finally taking this more seriously?

Then I sense the presence behind me and see that my giant bull mate is here. Of course they listen when he's around. Red mohawk, nose piercing, intense eyes, and freaking huge. The guy is a bit intimidating.

"My beloved, you missed lunch," he says as I turn to face him.

"I know. I've just been so busy. I really need them to do well tonight."

Okot and I watch as the cupids aim and fire their Love Arrows at the targets that Ronak installed. None of them hit their targets. Not one. The ball-gown-wearing chick doesn't even get hers to fly. It just falls at her feet, and she complains about blisters. The troll cupid keeps breaking his bow on account of his hands being so big. And thanks to the loincloth he's wearing, it's pretty obvious that *that* is pretty big, too. Every time he walks, his scrotum totem peeks out. But it's not a nice sight. It has warts on it. Also, it's furry. Note to self: Get this guy some freaking pants.

I face-palm. "You guys really suck at this," I call out.

"You're a right motivational speaker, you are," Sev jokes beside me.

"It's not funny, Sev," I say, lowering my voice. "None of them can shoot a damn arrow!"

He shrugs, unconcerned. "These are the flunkies. What did you expect?"

"I don't know."

Sev claps me on the back. "Don't worry, boss. At least they're fooking tryin' now. They weren't even doing that for their first training. I think they'll be an alrigh' bunch." He turns and points in my face. "But don't fooking tell 'em I said that."

I snort. "Your secret is safe with me."

I watch as Amorette toddles behind the cupids, looking like a general overseeing her troops. She's now traded in her wooden sword for a Love Arrow.

When one of the cupids misses his target again, Amorette shakes her head at him in dramatic disappointment. "You're real bad at this, mister."

The goth dude looks down at her with a scowl. "Whatever, kid. Why don't you go bug someone else?"

Amorette looks him right in the eye...and then stabs him in the calf with her Love Arrow.

Crying out in pain, he grabs his calf and hops around on his other leg. The arrow is protruding out of him, and I can already see a bloodstain leaking through his dark pants.

I wince and rush forward. "Crap. Amorette! That was very naughty!"

Amorette just blinks innocently.

Sev laughs. "Nice aim, kid."

"Oh my gosh, is that *blood*?" the ball gown chick shrieks. "I can't stand the sight of blood!" Then she faints.

The nerdy cupid catches her. Well, sort of. He lunges forward, his skinny arms swinging up, but he loses his footing so he mostly just breaks her fall.

The cell phone girl rolls her eyes and sighs. "Everyone is stupid."

Sev and I seem like experts compared to this lot.

The goth cupid, still hopping around in pain, falls on the ground with a grimace, staring at the Love Arrow with panic. "Someone take it out!"

"Don't worry," I tell him. I look over to Okot, only to realize he's already left and is walking back over with Evert in tow.

I kneel down to my deceivingly cute and innocent-looking daughter. "Amorette, we don't stab people with arrows. It's not nice."

She looks up at me with big puppy dog eyes. "He started it. Daddy Ro said if someone starts it, I can finish it."

"Of course he did," I mumble. "But you need to apologize, okay?"

She pouts. "Fine." She looks over at the cupid. "Sorry for stabbin' you."

He snorts. "Sure you are."

She continues to stare at him, her eyes narrowing.

He automatically leans away from her. "You're a violent little thing, aren't you?"

Her eyes flash genfin gold.

"Okay!" I say, quickly scooping her up. "Someone needs her nap."

Amorette pouts, but at least her eyes go back to normal. Well, *normal* might not be the right word since her eye color changes all the time. It's one of the reasons why it's so hard to tell which of my guys is her biological father. Her eyes look more like my lady luck prism of colors, constantly shifting shades. But her tantrums? Yeah, those are full genfin. She goes animal, growls at everyone, and then usually scratches her claws against the furniture.

I watch as Evert comes sauntering over. And when I say saunter, I mean it. The guy has some serious swagger going on. He's dressed in a loose black tunic with the ties undone at the top so that I can see some chest muscles, and when he walks, it's like he leads with his dick. It sounds weird, but it's totally hot. I get distracted watching him dick-walk toward me. I can't help it.

"Eyes up here, Scratch," he says, and I wrench my gaze from his crotch to his smirking face. "Cupid problems?"

I nod. "Our daughter stabbed him with a Love Arrow," I explain.

At first, Evert looks like he wants to laugh, but then a fierce frown comes over his face. Before I can react, he has a chokehold on the injured cupid, whose face goes from super pale to a mottled shade of purple.

"Evert! Stop!" I put Amorette down, trying to get him to stop.

"This fucker better not even *think* about falling in love with our daughter, or I'll pop his fucking head off right now."

"Oh my gods, can you knock it off? He isn't going to fall in love with her. It doesn't work that way," I tell him.

Evert loosens his hold, but only slightly, at least enough for the cupid to take a big sputtered breath. "Explain."

"She doesn't have cupid powers. And since she's the first ever *born* cupid, I don't know that she ever will. So until she does, she can't activate a Love Arrow," I tell him. "Just like you can't take one and shoot people up with love. It would just be a normal arrow for you, and until she starts developing cupid powers, the same goes for her, too."

Evert considers this for a moment and then lets go. Goth cupid coughs and falls over to his side, taking in haggard breaths. "Now I see where the kid gets her violent tendencies."

Instead of being embarrassed, Evert looks proud.

Evert kneels down in front of Amorette, but instead of lecturing her about the importance of not stabbing people, he smiles at her. "That was bloody brilliant. You nearly sunk it all the way to the bone. Your training lessons are working," he tells her.

Amorette beams.

"Evert," I hiss.

He looks up at me, oblivious. "What? You want me to shoot him in the other leg?"

87

"Yeah!" Amorette exclaims.

"*No*," I say sternly. "I want you to heal him."

Evert curls his lip. "Why?"

I give him *the look*. You know, the one that says I won't be petting his zoo anytime soon if he doesn't do what I ask.

He sighs. "Fine." He leans over the guy and, without giving any warning, yanks the arrow out of his leg. Gothy cries out and curses. All the other cupids look down at him with a mixture of pity and amusement.

"You could've warned me!" he snaps at Evert.

"Where's the fun in that?" Evert retorts. "Roll up your pants."

The cupid's face turns ashen, and he covers his crotch, like Evert just threatened to castrate him. "W-why?" he sputters. "She already explained the Love Arrow didn't make me fall in love with your daughter! I swear, I won't!"

"You're fucking right about that, asshole," Evert says. "But if you want me to heal you, roll up your damn pant leg so that I can see the wound. I'm not fucking touching you more than I have to."

The cupid looks to me, and I nod reassuringly.

Defeated, he grabs his pant leg and shoves it up where we can see the gaping, bloody wound.

"Eww," cellphone cupid says. "That's so gross."

Evert slaps his hand down on the guy's calf way harder than necessary, making him hiss in pain. His pained expression changes to relief when Evert's powers stitch his skin back together.

"There," Evert says, pushing off and standing back up.

Okot is ready with a water bucket for Evert to wash his hands with, and when he's done getting off all the blood, he scoops up Amorette and places her on his shoulders. "Let's go tell Daddy Ro all about this, and then see if Daddy Syl will carve you your own bow and arrow set, yeah?"

Amorette claps excitedly. "Yeah!"

"This is why she stabs people!" I call at his retreating back.

He just chuckles.

Like I said, we won't be winning any parenting awards anytime soon.

CHAPTER 16

The three coveys that are being bonded tonight are from very prominent families of high social standing. Two of the coveys have five males, and the third covey has four. The only problem? I'm picking up barely any affection from any of them. We have our work cut out for us.

Everything in the pavilion is decorated lavishly. Fairy lights and lanterns are lighting everything up, and white flowers are on every surface. At the center is a beautifully carved wooden archway set on a raised dais, with chairs for the audience circling around it.

It seems like the entire genfin population has shown up for these ceremonies. There have to be at least seven hundred people in attendance. I'm standing in the back with my cupid trainees and Sev, trying to give them some last-minute pep talks.

"As soon as I give you the signal, I'll push you into the Veil, and you can get to work. Remember, Flirt-Touches first. We wanna get them nice and saturated."

Sev pulls a face as he puffs on a pipe with the

motorcycle-club looking cupid. "Don't say *saturated*, boss. It sounds fooking weird."

"You sound weird," I snap. Then I instantly feel bad. "Sorry, Sev. You don't sound weird. Actually, I think your accent is hot."

Sev practically throws the pipe at motorcycle cupid before sidling up beside me. Tossing an arm over my shoulders, he pulls me close. "You finally ready to bring me into the fold, then, boss? I'll be a right fooking treat to ya."

Of course, that's when my mates come up. Ronak doesn't say anything. He just calmly walks forward, takes hold of Sev's arm that's still draped around me, and lifts it up...while squeezing him so hard I can hear his bones groan in protest.

Sev flinches and yowls in pain. "Fooking bloody boaby! That hurts!"

Ronak releases him, and Sev steps back to a safe distance away from me. "Bloody fooking hell, boss. He's a right scunner, ain't he?" he asks, rubbing his injured arm.

"Don't touch my mate," Ronak says simply.

Sev smiles. "Aye, I see why you like these males, boss. Must make you right hot when they go all alpha on ya, am I right? I'd love to get in on the action," he says, wagging his eyebrows.

"I'm gonna fucking maim you one of these days," Evert tells him.

Sev's grin widens. He turns to me and threads his fingers together beseechingly. "Oh, come on, boss. Lemme join your harem, aye? I'm gantin' for it. This hate talk is the bloody best foreplay I've had in weeks. Your mates are practically beggin' for some Sev."

Okot frowns at him. Sylred shakes his head. Ronak

and Evert look like they're silently communicating with each other about who's gonna murder him and how they can hide it from me. Sev is just too much of a shit-stirrer for his own good. He absolutely lives for irritating my mates. He must have some kind of death wish.

"Sev?" I say.

"Yeah, boss?"

"Shut up."

"Right-o, boss."

"Okay, listen up," I tell the cupids, making them gather around. "It's almost showtime. You guys know what to do. We just have to jumpstart the genfins and make them go into heat; that way, they can form a bond. And, if we shoot them up with some well-timed Love Arrows, we might even get them to like each other by the end of the night."

A few of the cupids snicker.

"If you do this, then you'll officially pass training, and you'll be ready to start Love Matches for Valentine's Day on Earth. And if you don't screw that up, I'll reward you with an extra vacation day. Deal?"

"Can we have sex during vacation?"

"Have at it."

The cupid trainees all nod approvingly. See? Even the flunkies can do well once they have the proper motivation. I guess the possibility of orgasms is the right incentive. I'll have to add that to the new cupid trainee handbook.

Elder Mortel comes up, looking a bit frazzled. "Everyone is here," he tells us, breaching the group. "Are your employees ready?"

"Yep," I say confidently.

Elder Mortel looks away from me to size up my

cupids...and immediately frowns. His eyes go over the goths, the nerdy guy who sounds like he needs an inhaler, the ball gown chick fighting with the cellphone holder, and his eyes widen in horror when he takes in the troll.

"These are your cupids?"

I nod and try to get his eyes back on me. He doesn't look away until the troll starts picking his nose with a Love Arrow. I motion to Sev, and he immediately kicks the troll in the shin. "Fooking knock it off, get it?"

The troll puts his booger-laden arrow back in his quiver. I gag a little.

"Erm...right..." The elder looks more and more doubtful. "Maybe this isn't a good idea..."

"No," I rush to explain. "They can totally do this. I promise." I think. Maybe.

He regards me dubiously. "If you're sure..."

Nope. Not at all. "Yep. I'm positive." I smile.

Elder Mortel sighs. "Alright. The ceremony is starting, so whenever you're ready."

I nod, and he walks away, leaving us alone again. I notice all the hundreds of genfins that have come to watch are now finding their seats, dusk is quickly turning to a beautiful starry night, and the coveys to be mated are taking their places on the dais.

"Alright. Showtime," I tell my cupids. "This is your only chance to impress me and pass training. Please don't screw this up. You all know who your marks are, and you've already paired up. Work together. Remember, being a cupid takes finesse. You can't just go slapping people with Flirt-Touches and tossing out Love. Timing is everything. Let them warm up to each other first with plenty of desire, but don't make it so they're getting

94

hardies on stage for all of their families to see. Hone in on your inner cupid. You got this."

"In other words, don't fook this up, ya miserable shites," Sev puts in. He's helpful like that.

I hear Elder Mortel begin speaking on the dais, announcing the covey names and declaring the mate matches.

"Sev? You'll watch them in the Veil while they work?"

"Aye."

"Alright then. Good luck."

A huge glowing rainbow appears above us, ending in a pot of gold at my feet.

You'd think I'd learn by now. Hell, heaven, luck—those words should be stricken from my vocabulary, but things just slip out.

My guys stare down at it, while all seven hundred genfins in attendance look over at me and the nighttime rainbow that should definitely not be here.

"It's fine!" I call out. "Please continue!"

Elder Mortel pulls his eyes away from the scene and clears his throat distractedly. "Right. As I was saying..."

"Alright, go on."

Using my cupid boss powers, I push the cupids into the Veil and hope for the best.

"What are the chances that they're going to totally screw this up and it'll end in disaster?" I ask, watching the dais anxiously.

"I'd say a good fifty-fifty chance," Evert drawls while digging through the pot of gold. "Here," he says, flipping me a golden coin. "For luck."

I try to catch it, but the damn thing bounces off my boobs and then falls down the top of my dress. Evert smirks.

"Did you do that on purpose?" I ask, trying to dig a hand down my bodice so I can retrieve it.

"Does that sound like something I'd do?" he counters.

"Pretty much, yeah."

He smirks. "Need help getting it out?" he asks with a cock of his brow.

I keep digging in there, but let's face it, there's a lot going on in the boobage department. Also, I'm pretty sure my nipples just started leaking milk. I sigh and give up. "I'll find it later."

It's not the first time I've lost something in my cleavage, and it won't be the last.

CHAPTER 17

"*H*oly fooking baws, the little shiteheads aren't completely useless, aye?"

I'm watching the ceremony like a hawk. Sev is rotating them out on my orders, while I whisper instructions from our spot beside the dais. Since they'll be doing most of their work in the Veil, it's best to have them practice there now.

Elder Mortel gave us a little alcove to use that's close enough to see what's happening, without being too near to be distracting. Except, you know, the troll-cupid who's pretty much distracting no matter where he's standing. I keep him in the Veil.

I have to admit, so far, everything is going well, and we've only had a few hiccups. The first was when the nerdy cupid accidentally tripped at the start of the ceremony. He caught himself on the genfin female's boobs. Her soon-to-be mates weren't happy. I pushed him back into the Veil before they could clobber him.

Then, ball gown cupid went and blew *way* too much

Lust at the first covey during their ceremony. At least two of the males came in their trousers. There were wet spots.

But, with my help, all ten of those genfins were successfully hit with Love Arrows. When I say hit, I mean they were pretty much shanked by my trainees, since shooting with a bow is still too expert level for them. But hey, cupid baby steps. And anyway, the cupids were in the Veil, so no genfin was harmed during the Love Arrow shanking. In fact, they went from only slightly sharing affection for each other to having some solid desire and tenderness.

Now, we're down to the last covey.

"Alright," I say, giving whispered instructions to cell phone cupid and goth cupid. "Your team members primed this covey up really well. All you have to do is seal the deal with Love Arrows," I tell them.

Goth cupid is a bit arrow shy since Amorette stabbed him, but I hand him a full quiver and pat him on the shoulder. "You got this."

He holds it as far away from himself as he can. Cell phone cupid rolls her eyes and sighs at him. "Such a newb."

"Okay, go on," I say, and then I push them into the Veil.

The other cupids and I watch the covey as they go through the rituals being led by the elder. As the vows are exchanged, I put out my cupid senses. Even though I can't see them in the Veil, I feel it the moment a Love Arrow hits its mark.

Love pulses in the air, and all of the trainees standing with me visibly shudder from it. I smile when I take in the expressions of the genfins on the dais. The males' expressions soften on their female, and she loses some of her nervous tension and relaxes under their touch when they clasp hands.

"Okay, you two," I say, pointing to the troll and the cupid in the leather getup. "You guys are up. After they drink out of the ceremonial chalice, blow some Lust at them."

As soon as the cupids nod in understanding, I push them into the Veil.

"I think you actually fooking managed it, boss. You managed to train this lot, after all," Sev says in an impressed tone. I'd be a bit offended if I weren't surprised myself.

"Thanks, Sev," I say, my eyes facing forward.

I feel the Lust leaking out at the dais, and I sigh a bit in relief. This is actually turning out alright. Then I feel a bit more Lust. And more. And more. And...

"Shit!" I whisper-hiss. "Sev, the damn troll is breathing too much out!"

"On it," Sev says before disappearing into a puff of pink.

I watch anxiously, but it's pretty much too late. The troll cupid must have breathed way too much of the stuff, and considering he's so big, it's leaking out over the entire gathered audience.

I wince at the change of the genfins in the seats. Simultaneous purring breaks out. Tails are obscenely wrapped around mates. Hardies are clearly visible. I'm pretty sure a few people with front row seats moan.

The genfin males on the stage cut Elder Mortel short when they down the rest of the contents in the chalice and then toss the female over their shoulder to hustle her off the stage. She giggles in delight as the five of them run off to go nest for the heat that has clearly been jump-started.

"Good grieving hearts," I mutter.

Sev pops back next to me along with the troll and the leather cupid. I place my hands on my hips and shake my head. The troll looks down at his feet. "Sorry, miss boss."

"Just be more careful next time."

"Yes, miss boss."

I blow out a breath and look back to the rest of the cupids, flinging my arms up. "Well, that was completely, utterly, totally…" They all cringe as my words taper off. I grin. "Fantastic."

The cupids' eyes flash to mine, and I see the relief spread across the group. "You guys did so well for your first assignment. Apart from the few mishaps, I'm confident that you guys will do great on Earth for Valentine's Day."

"Really?" the nerdy guy asks, pushing his glasses up his nose.

"Really. I'm very proud of you all."

I can tell they don't want to like my praise, but a few smiles escape, anyway.

"You can have the rest of the night off here," I say, and I get a collection of whoops and claps. "I'll send you back to Earth tomorrow. Make it the best Valentine's Day ever for those humans, alright?"

They all nod and break off, while Sev and I stay behind.

Sev bumps me playfully with his shoulder. "Good fooking job, you."

"Thanks, Sev. I couldn't have done it without you."

"We're alrigh' at this love shite after all, aye?"

I smile. "Aye."

And yeah, we might have seven hundred genfins around with boners and wet undies, but it's a small price to pay for three new, happy genfin matches.

Cupid boss win.

y mates and I have been celebrating at the after-party for hours. The pavilion quickly changed from the formal, elegant mating ceremony to a lavish, slightly weird genfin revelry. There's a lot of... rutting going on. It's been confirmed that the new mated coveys successfully went into heat, so they're all sequestered away in their homes, nesting and getting it on. As far as the rest of the partygoers? Well, the troll cupid let out a lot of lust. The sexfest was pretty much inevitable.

"I'm officially on maternity leave," I muse aloud.

The four of my guys are settled around me in a nice mate cocoon while we watch the entertainment and enjoy the food. There are genfins on the stage doing their ritual dances while music plays in the background. More genfins come around with wooden platters, serving kabob-style food and fairy wine. It's a beautiful night, even amidst all the animal grunting going on around us.

"Yes. You worked hard, and you trained them well,"

Sylred tells me, kissing me on the top of the head. "I'm proud of you."

"Thanks, Syl."

I'm sandwiched between him and Evert, while I'm using Okot as a chair, and Ronak has my legs in his lap. Everyone is lounging on furs and pillows on the ground since genfins can't handle tables and chairs in their animal forms.

My cupids are enjoying themselves with the rest of the night off, chatting up genfins and probably trying to get lucky. Sev disappeared hours ago with a male and female in tow, the horny bastard.

Just then, Ronak's mother walks up with her mates. She looks down at us where we sit, but instead of seeming haughty like usual, she's regarding me curiously. "Well. It seems you being a cupid was slightly helpful to genfins, after all. You didn't completely embarrass yourself for once," she says.

I beam. "That's the nicest thing you've ever said to me!" I bet it was all the Lust she involuntarily inhaled. I'm pretty sure I saw her sneaking off with her mates earlier.

She sniffs. "Yes, well. About that thing that you mentioned earlier."

I blink at her with confusion until I remember my offer to shoot her and her males up with some Love Arrows. "Oh! Yes," I say eagerly. "What about it?"

"It would be quite alright if you tried it. Sometime. When I'm not much too busy for you."

My grin widens. I feel like I just won a medal. My cupids and I must have really impressed her tonight. "Just say the word, and I'll be there."

She sniffs again and then gives me a terse nod. "Well, then. I bid you all good night." She looks to Ronak. "Don't allow your covey to embarrass the Fircrown name tonight."

Ronak opens his mouth to argue, but Evert's chuckle cuts him off. "Don't worry, Resha. We'll wait until tomorrow to do that."

She sniffs displeasedly and then walks off. Ronak's fathers shake their heads, tell us goodnight, and follow behind her.

I turn to my mates in victory. "See!" I say excitedly. "She totally likes me now. I knew I could finally get her. By this time next year, we'll totally be getting pedicures together and primping each other's wings while we gossip. She's gonna like me so much she'll probably even learn how to smile."

"Let's not get crazy with the expectations," Evert says dryly.

I tilt my head. "You're right. Smiling is a bit much."

"I'm proud of you," Ronak says, running his callused hands up and down my legs. "Coming from my mother, that was practically a hug. You tamed the old witch. I didn't think it was possible."

"I'm super good at impossible things."

"Yes, you are," Okot says behind me, slipping my hair over my shoulder so he can kiss the back of my neck. I hum in pleasure. His lips send soft caresses down my spine, and I shiver in response.

"Mossie has Amorette all night tonight," I say.

Ronak's black eyes connect with mine. "Yes."

"That means we can have super sexy times without worrying we'll be interrupted," I point out.

Evert immediately jumps to his feet, jolting me a little. We all look up at him in surprise. "What the hell are you fuckers waiting for? Let's get our mate home," he demands.

I laugh, but the other guys rush into action. Okot carries me all the way to the carriage and keeps me on his lap when we get in it.

With all of them sitting in such close quarters, I take a deep breath, and then I Lust-Breath the shit out of them.

All four of them groan. The carriage is filled with pink Lust-Breath curling around us, and I giggle when their pants instantly tent.

"You little demon," Ronak rebukes, trying to adjust his pants. "What have we told you about Lusting us?"

"Not to do it unless I'm ready to face the consequences," I say with a coy smile.

"That's right. You're in trouble now."

A thrill travels down me, landing directly onto my core. I grin flirtatiously. "Good. Because I want you to teach me lots and lots of lessons."

CHAPTER 19

$\mathcal{I}$ shift against Okot's huge erection digging into my ass, and his fingers dig into my waist as he groans.

"Now she's teasing the fucking lamassu," Evert smirks. He's not doing anything to hide his erection. Instead, he leans back farther against the carriage wall, jutting his hips toward me. I try to lean in to touch, but Ronak's hand shoots out, and his fingers wrap around my wrist.

"Nope. You don't get to touch."

I pout. "That's not nice."

Ronak smirks. "Should've thought about that before, little demon. You broke the rules, so now your teasing ass is ours." He leans in close, his beard scratching against my neck and ear. "We are going to fill you up and make you scream."

Gods, I think my panties just spontaneously combusted.

"Besides, we have something to show you. And if you start getting frisky now, you'll be too distracted."

I cock my head, and my brows crease together. "What is it?"

"It's a surprise," he says, and it's clear from his voice that I won't be getting anything else out of them.

When the carriage rolls up to our den, I practically fly out of there. I'm so ready for their mysterious surprise, and to be sexed up, it's not even funny.

They help me down the stairs and into our den, and as soon as I step inside, I gasp in shock.

"Holy heartbeat," I breathe.

I look around in complete awe at our den. There are white candles *everywhere*. On the floor and on every flat surface, there are hundreds of them, making the entire den glow. Then, there's the red rose petals. They're sprinkled throughout the floor, making a trail between the candle walkway leading to the bedroom. On the wall is a huge red heart, carved out of wood and painted red, with the words "Be Our Valentine" carved into it.

My eyes fill with tears as I turn to them. "You...you did all this for me?"

They all nod. "We had some help," Sylred explains. "But we heard what you said, about why you loved Valentine's Day so much. We wanted you to know that even if we don't always say it, we *do* love and cherish you, every single day."

"I love you too," I whisper, my voice choked up. I wrap my hands around each of them in turn and kiss them on their lips. "Thank you," I say. "This was so nice and romantic and just...perfect." I smile at them. "You're the best mates in any realm, ever."

"You deserve it all, my beloved," Okot says.

"She does deserve it all," Evert says, wagging his brows

to make me know he means something of the sexual variety. Now I'm even hornier than before.

"You guys are gonna get sexually rewarded for this romantic gesture," I tell them honestly.

Without wasting any time, I turn on my heel and hurry down rose petal lane, all the way to the bedroom. As soon as I get inside, I'm already trying to undo my bodice ties to my dress. I sigh in frustration when the ties get tangled.

"Hurry! Someone help me get naked so you can teach me lots of lessons and give me orgasms," I tell them.

Evert smirks as he steps forward to undo the dress for me, but when it takes too long, he says, "Fuck it," and swipes his claws down the back. My dress falls in a heap on the floor...along with the coin that was stuck in my cleavage.

I frown. "You ruined my new dress."

He shrugs apologetically as his blue eyes rake over my exposed breasts. "We'll buy you a new one. I wanted you naked, and I wasn't going to wait."

"Okay." I nod immediately, because I'm really liking his logic.

Then, Evert kneels in front of me, and I get all excited, thinking he's about to press my beaverbutton with his tongue, but the fucker blows a huge breath of Lust right at my clit instead.

I come on the spot.

Ronak catches me when my knees give out. Evert stands back up with a smirk.

"Y-You fucker," I pant.

He shrugs. "That's what you get for teasing us in the carriage."

I'm not gonna lie, it's a fantastic punishment. Not that I'll admit it.

But now I really need some dick. Like, pronto. My vagina is practically snapping her lips in impatience.

Ronak gives the guys some weird alpha looks to communicate, and the next thing I know, I'm on the bed, and they're stripping.

"Gods, we haven't been able to do this all together for months," I say, my eyes raking over their bodies. Sylred is the slenderest, but he's still larger than me and has a nicely toned and tanned body. In contrast, Evert and Okot are pale, but they also have drool-worthy bodies. Okot just happens to be huge. Ronak, of course, has muscles on muscles on muscles. But all four of them have those delicious Vs pointing down to the promised lands. It's become my favorite letter.

When their shirts and pants are discarded, I hungrily eye their cocks. I also drool a little. I don't think they notice.

"Looks like she's ready to suck a cock," Evert smirks.

Dammit. They noticed.

"Whose turn is it?" I ask, probably a bit too eagerly, because the guys chuckle.

Ronak considers my question for a moment, and then nods at Okot. "It's his turn for your mouth."

I grimace a bit. Not because I don't like sucking him, but because he's so freaking huge that I nearly unhinged my jaw last time. Okot notices my apprehension. "You don't have to do anything you don't want to do, my beloved."

Well, now I really want to. But first...

"Oh! Hold that thought. You guys are all here and hard, and I keep meaning to do this."

I sit back on my knees and then scramble for the nightstand. "Everyone stay where you are," I order as I root through the drawer. I can feel their eyes on my ass where I'm bending over.

When I find what I'm looking for, I immediately rush into action. I walk over to Sylred first, hold the measuring tape up to his dick, and spread it out. I hum in approval to myself at the number, and then I proceed to move onto Evert's, Ronak's, and then Okot's erections.

"What...what the fuck is happening?" Evert asks incredulously.

All four of my mates are watching me, bewildered.

When I see Okot's number, my eyebrows shoot up. I look over at Sylred since he's the carpenter of the bunch. "What's twenty fae forns converted to Earth realm inches?"

Sylred blinks at me. "I...I don't know."

"Hmm," I say thoughtfully. "Oh, well."

Now that I'm done, I return the measuring tape to the nightstand drawer in satisfaction. "Okay, all done," I say proudly.

My mates are looking at me, totally baffled.

"Did you just measure our dicks?" Ronak asks.

"Yep. I've just been waiting for the opportunity."

Evert snorts, and Sylred is biting on his lips, trying not to laugh. Ronak pinches the bridge of his nose. Okot looks smug, to be honest. But the guy with the biggest dick always does.

"Are you done now?" Ronak asks.

"Yeah. And I gotta say *very* impressive, guys. Really," I tell them, because it's always nice to compliment their cocks. Especially when they're standing at attention just for me.

Ronak shakes his head at me. "Little demon?"

"Yes, Alpha?" I ask coyly, and I see his dick twitch in response. He loves it when I call him that.

"Get your ass back on the bed."

I smile. "Yes, Alpha."

I immediately crawl back onto the bed and position myself in front of Okot. I reach up and grip him with both hands. My fingers can't wrap all the way around him, and both of my hands, one on top of the other, don't reach the end of him. There's still a good four inches left for me to suck. It's pierced and hard and beautiful, just waiting for me.

I lower my head and lick the tip, and Okot's hands immediately come up to cradle my head. His cock is so impressive. And sexy. The piercings just do something to me. I lean in against his groin and snuggle my face against the base of his cock, just to show it some love.

"Did she just nuzzle his cock?" Sylred asks.

"Yup," Evert chirps.

Sorry, not sorry.

When I open my mouth and start sucking on the head of his cock, Okot groans and his fingers press lightly into my scalp. Then I feel Ronak's bearded mouth latch onto my pussy from behind me, and I jolt in surprise.

"Hold still, Scratch. We'll take care of that itch for you," Evert says into my ear as he and Sylred come up on either side of me.

I immediately reach out to grab their dicks instead, both of which are hard and waiting for me. As soon as I wrap my hands around them, I squeeze firmly, eliciting groans from both directions.

"Can't go any deeper than that on the fucking lamas-su?" Evert asks.

I take it as a personal challenge.

I concentrate on the massive pierced cock in my mouth and open up wider so I can move my head lower on him.

"Good girl. You like sucking his big cock, don't you?" Evert says as he reaches over to fondle my breasts. I swear, my pussy starts crying tears of dirty-talk joy.

Still behind me, Ronak distracts me when his tongue moves over my clit teasingly, and then he starts lapping at my cupid canoochie like it's his favorite treat.

When his tongue starts spearing into me, I pop off Okot's cock and cry out in pleasure. "Oh, gods!"

"Nope, just us," Evert quips.

An orgasm shoots through me as Ronak continues to flick his tongue over my clit. When I'm coming down from the high, Ronak sits back and wipes his mouth and beard with the back of his arm.

He gives me a smirk full of male satisfaction. "I think our mate is ready."

"Yep. Totally ready," I pant, my body still rippling with my first orgasm.

They do their whole silent communication thing again, and then I'm repositioned until I'm on top of Sylred, his cock sliding into my pussy.

"Syl," I cry out, loving the feel of him inside of me. He leans up and kisses me, and then I feel Evert behind me, dripping oil down the crack of my ass. When I break away from Sylred's lips, I look over my shoulder to see Evert with hooded blue eyes. I watch hungrily as he fists himself, spreading the oil slowly over his shaft. It's so fucking sexy.

"You like watching, Scratch?" Evert says, his voice full of lust.

"Yeah."

Sylred rolls his hips underneath me, and I close my eyes in pleasure.

"Eyes on us, beautiful," Ronak's voice orders, and my eyes immediately flicker open.

Sylred lies back down, and Ronak and Okot come up on either side of me. Okot kisses me first. His tongue teases against mine, flicking it as he coaxes me into his delicious warmth. I breathe him in at the same time, and his intoxicating mate scent envelops me. It makes me dazed, and when he pulls away, I'm even more ready than I was a minute ago.

I can feel Evert behind me, teasing a finger into my ass, and I automatically clench up.

Sylred groans. "Fuck, sweetheart."

"Relax," Evert coaxes, running a gentle hand up my spine. "We'll take care of you."

"I know," I say, because it's true. They always take care of me.

When Evert starts pushing his cock into my ass, I feel Okot's fingers come down on my clit, while Ronak further distracts me by gripping my jaw firmly and crashing my lips against his.

Ecstasy. Full, complete, and solid ecstasy.

That's what it's like to be touched by all four of my mates. Sylred and Evert work together in tandem to keep their cocks in the perfect rhythm inside of me. Okot's fingers dance over my clit, tempting my body to breach the brink of orgasm again. And Ronak kisses the fuck out of me. He kisses exactly the same way he does everything else. His kiss is intense. Demanding. Rough. Sexy as fuck.

When Evert and Sylred move in a particular way, I have to wrench away from Ronak and cry out. "Oh my gods, you guys are doing some solid hip thrusts. Really, top notch work down there," I pant out.

I hear someone chuckle.

I lick my lips. "Okay. I'm ready for more, big bull," I tell Okot.

I lean forward as much as my pregnant belly will allow, and take him into my mouth again, and this time, I practically unhinge my jaw and try to take him as far back as I possibly can. He makes a deep grumbled sound of pleasure that fills me with pride and heat.

Ronak takes my hand and brings it to his hard and waiting cock, and I follow the rhythm he sets as I squeeze him hard. I feel him purr against my hand, and I go harder.

When my jaw needs a break from Okot's python, I switch over to Ronak. Back and forth I go, getting really sloppy with the spit, but I know it drives the guys wild, because their movements become even more erratic.

I shove my hands against their hips to get them to come closer. Then I fist both of their cocks toward my outstretched tongue and start stroking them hard and fast while keeping my tongue lapping against the heads of their cocks.

"Fucking hell," Evert groans behind me. "Look at her. Slurping and hand fucking both of them."

He sounds super proud. I preen a little.

Evert reaches around so my clit can get some attention again, and I moan against Ronak's and Okot's cocks.

"I'm gonna come," I whimper.

"Then finish us, little demon."

I smile up at him, my lips swollen and shining with saliva. "Yes, Alpha."

He growls with hunger.

I press my lips against their cocks again, a hand on each of their shafts, and then I blow Lust all over their dicks.

I've barely finished exhaling before they're coming, and I tilt my head up, feeling their ropes of cum landing on my neck and chest.

"Holy fuck, that was hot."

Evert and Sylred start pounding into me, and two different hands are teasing my clit. My body soars higher and higher, and with every stroke of Evert's and Sylred's cocks, I get closer to the peak.

When two mouths enclose over my nipples, their hot, rough hands kneading my sensitive flesh, I come hard, screaming something unintelligible, and my pussy tightens so much that I take Sylred and then Evert with me.

I keep repeating all four of their names over and over without a breath in between, while also switching to a garbled "Oh my gods" and "I super really love your cocks."

I can't help it.

When I'm coherent again, I realize that they've laid me on my side, Evert still behind me and Sylred in front. Their cocks are still buried inside of me, and my pussy is still rippling with aftershocks of pleasure.

Okot is at my feet, while my head rests on Ronak's thigh, and his fingers are threading through my hair lovingly. My mates cuddle me like this after sex, showing me every time how much they adore me.

"I love you guys," I tell them.

"And we love you," they all say in perfect unison.

I smile against Ronak's muscled thigh.

"At least she said she loved *us* this time," Evert points out. "She's usually talking to our dicks after sex."

"I love your cocks, too," I say honestly.

I feel Evert twitch inside of me, already gearing up for round two. Which apparently, I'm down for, because I feel myself getting wet.

Like, really wet.

I jolt upright. "Oh my gods!"

I push them off me and scramble off the bed, watching in horror as liquid drips down my thighs. And yeah, there's a lot of cum, but this liquid is clear. And it's gushing. It looks like Old Faithful just erupted from my vagina.

Everyone freezes as we watch a ridiculous amount of liquid explode out of me.

My terrified, wide eyes lift up to them.

"Either my vagina just sprouted a geyser or my water just broke."

CHAPTER 20

It took precisely two minutes for my mates to clean up, get dressed, and put me into the tub. I'm now clean, and my vagina has stopped spewing out liquid, so that's good. What's not good? The fact that my contractions hit, and I am in total fucking agony.

I've been moved to the bed, the genfin midwife is here, and all four of my mates are in the bedroom, trying to tend to me.

I'm walking in circles in our bedroom, wearing nothing but a loose nightdress, clinging onto Ronak's arms as he walks backwards with me, keeping me steady.

I'm panting, my pink hair is plastered against my forehead, and my red wings keep popping in and out.

"This. Fucking. Sucks!" I yell through clenched teeth.

I stop walking as yet another contraction hits, leaning over until my face is smashed against Ronak's arm. When it gets particularly painful, I open my mouth and bite down on Ronak's arm with a scream.

A pained grunt escapes him, but that's all. The poor

guy doesn't even try to get his arm away from my teeth. He just takes it. That's strength right there.

When the contraction ends, I finally release his flesh and lean back up. "Oh gods. That was a bad one. I kinda hate you all right now. So much. I wanna punch you. Also them. Oh, you're bleeding."

Ronak and I look at his mangled skin. There are very clear teeth marks decorating his forearm, with blood beading up.

"Sorry," I say guiltily. "I love you. I d-didn't mean to *hurt* you!" Now I'm sobbing.

Ronak shakes his head. "It's okay, little demon. You're in pain."

"I know b-but I don't wa-want you to b-be in pain, too!" I cry.

Then another contraction hits.

"Oh, shit, shit, shit!" I cringe, squeezing my eyes shut tight as I brace against Ronak again. "I swear to all the freaking shits in all the fucking fae realms, I hate you and your perfect stupid fucking dicks!" I yell. "I will tie your cocks into a noose and hang you all if you ever try to have sex with me again!"

My entire body clamps down like I'm having three million period cramps combined at one time and, yeah. "I'm pretty sure I'm gonna die."

"You're not going to die, my beloved," Okot tells me, and I feel him petting my sweat-drenched hair. "Would you like to bite my arm next?"

"Aww, you're so sweet," I gasp.

"*And* her contraction is over," Evert smirks, the amusement evident in his tone.

I straighten up from my hunched position, and the midwife immediately fusses over me. She just plops a squat right between my legs where I stand, lifts up my nightdress, and checks things down under. I don't even care. She already saw everything there was to see when I gave birth to Amorette. I pretty much lost all modesty once she rifled through my whiskerwallet and helped stretch out my love lips. There's just no coming back from that.

"Drink this," she says, passing me another tonic of who-the-heck-knows-what mixed with those damn poppleberries.

"These stupid poppleberries don't help at all," I complain right before I down it all in one swig.

"It does help," she tells me sternly. I want to rip her eyebrows off.

She blinks at me and covers her brows. Oh. I guess I said that out loud.

Before I can apologize, another contraction takes over, and I'm right back to cursing, screaming, and unintentionally inflicting pain on my mates. When the pain gets so bad that I start hissing through my teeth, I take the glass cup and hurl it against the wall. I hear a very satisfying sound of glass shattering.

When the haze of pain ebbs away at the end of the contraction, I open my eyes and blink over at the broken glass. "Whoops."

"It's alright, my beloved," Okot assures me.

"It was a good throw," Ronak says behind me, looking oddly proud. Weird alpha male.

I realize that I'm now being supported by Evert and Sylred. The guys keep tagging out. I notice that Ronak's arm is now bandaged. So is Okot's finger. And Sylred's cheek. Wow. I really do a number on these guys.

But I can't be held responsible. Not when it feels like

121

my body is trapped in some cruel version of a Chinese finger trap.

"Oh gods, it hurts. It hurts!" I groan, shifting my weight from side to side as I brace against the wall. Someone is rubbing my back. Too softly. Way too softly.

"Harder!" I snap.

Hands start kneading into my knotted and tense muscles as I try to breathe in and out. "That's too hard!" I complain at the massaging hands. "Stop touching me wrong!"

The hands immediately go away.

So. Much. Pain.

"Get it out! Get it out!" I scream at the room.

"You will," Sylred assures me.

"No. *You* get it out! Be useful! Don't just stand there!"

"She's ready to push," I hear the midwife say.

I straighten up again and whirl around on my heels like I'm going to fight her off. "No! I'm not ready! I don't wanna push!"

"You have to," the genfin female tells me gently.

"Gimme some more *popplefuckinberries!*"

She shakes her head at me. "You cannot have more than you've already had."

I'm pretty sure I make a keening sound before making up some new swear words that aren't completely coherent. I also may or may not accidentally threaten her life.

"Come on, honey, let's get you onto the bed," the midwife croons, "so you can start pushing."

"Don't make me," I sob.

Ronak comes in front of me and takes my face in his hands. "You can do this," he tells me.

I shake my head. "I've been having contractions for hours and *hours*, all because your stupidly well-endowed

122

cocks make me go into labor! I'm so tired. And it hurts. And I can't. I just can't, Ronak. I don't have it in me," I whimper, feeling the tears drip down my cheeks. I'm so incredibly tired and terrified that my entire body starts to shake, and my eyes shut as panic closes in on me.

"Look at me," Ronak says in his strong, sure voice. My eyes lift to his, and I stare into his black irises, focusing on the steady tone of his voice. "You are persistent. You have done impossible things. You saved an entire realm. You saved us. You're strong. And you can do this. You hear me, mate?" he asks, his touch firm against my jaw. "You. Can. Do. This."

I nod and take a shaky breath.

"Then let's get you onto the bed, and soon, we can meet our baby."

My face crumples, and he wipes away my tears with the pads of his thumbs.

With his help, I make my way onto the bed, which is covered with extra padding for the birth and to make sure our mattress is protected from all the incoming fluids.

When Ronak starts to help me sit down, I squeeze his hand. "I need you all," I say desperately. "Don't leave."

He looks me steadily in the eye. "Never."

Ronak nods to the guys, and they take their places. I sit on the bed between Okot's legs, my back resting against his chest. Ronak takes my right side, while Evert is on my left, and Sylred stays beside Evert, rubbing my feet and aching legs.

The midwife settles at the foot of the bed and checks me. Her furry brown wings are tucked neatly at her back, and her hair is pulled into a tight bun. "Okay, dear. Next contraction, I want you to push."

So I do.

Again and again and a-fucking-gain.

Until finally...

I collapse back against Okot, my chest heaving.

"What is it?" I ask, watching as the midwife gathers the baby. The telltale sound of an infant cry erupts in the room, and I smile tiredly at the sound. All four of my mates simultaneously tense up with nervousness and excitement as they strain to see the baby.

The midwife lifts the baby up to me, and I see the second most adorable face I've ever seen in my life, after Amorette.

"A little girl," the midwife declares proudly.

"Genfin tail?" Ronak asks.

The midwife turns the baby so we can see. "Pink hair like her mama, but no genfin tail," the midwife answers. "She has red-ringed eyes. She's a lamassu."

I feel Okot tense behind me, and then Ronak does some crazy alpha handling business stuff, and Okot moves from behind me and gets up from the bed to take the baby.

The beaming midwife passes her over, and Okot takes her in his huge arms, cradling her like she's the most precious, fragile thing in all the realms. Tears fall from my eyes at the expression of wonder on his face.

"Hello, little love," he says to her, and her own cries instantly dry up.

Her tiny hand wraps around his finger, and Okot smiles. He looks up at me, and our eyes lock, my heart near bursting when I see his wet with joy.

"Thank you, my beloved," he whispers in total reverence.

I bite my shaking lip and taste the salty tears that drip down.

The other guys move to get a look at our sweet new baby girl, cooing words of adoration.

"Alright, let's get this afterbirth delivered," the midwife says, but I'm already contracting, and I cry out from the intense pain that takes me by surprise.

The midwife hurries between my legs, but I'm already pushing. The guys scramble around me, confused. The midwife looks up from my hoo-ha and beams. "There's another baby!"

I blink at her. "Come again?"

She nods. "Twins! You're having twins! You need to push!"

Cocklehearts in a cottonhole. I'm gonna kill someone.

CHAPTER 21

I look at the midwife like she's insane. Also like I want to murder her with my demon powers. I seriously consider soul-sucking her for, like, a good thirty seconds.

"You've got to push, honey," she tells me again.

I shake my head. "I...I just..." I point at the baby I just delivered. "I already did that! I'm supposed to be done! That's the rules!"

"Yes, but now you're going to do it again. Now push!"

"*Fuuuuuuuuucking hell*!" I scream as I push as hard as I can.

Of course, that's when the demon Jerkahf appears in a burst of hellfire smoke.

He materializes at the foot of my bed, with a front row seat to my stretched-out uppercunt.

When we see each other, our eyes widen, and we both shriek in alarm.

"Don't look at me!" I shriek at the same time that he cries, "My eyes!"

Evert is on him in a hot second, smashing his fist

against the demon's jaw, but I'm too busy to intervene because I'm pushing again and feeling like my vagina is stretching wide enough to accommodate a freaking elephant.

It's so hard. It hurts. My entire vagina is on fire. "Something isn't right!" I wail. "Oh gods, it's too big!"

The midwife has a strained look on her face as she tries to help me pry the baby from my body. "Keep pushing!" she urges.

I push and push and push until black spots appear in my vision, and then...a baby bull pops out of me.

The midwife holds it up in shock. Its sleek hair is covered in blood and placenta. I pant, and everyone freezes in astonishment, looking at the freaking bull that I just pushed out of my vagina. It has little baby horns— dulled, thank gods—and little hooves. Oh, and its wings? They're cupid red. It's adorable, but...

My eyes swing to my lamassu mate. "You...you didn't tell me that I might have to give birth to a freaking winged *bull*!" I screech.

He looks at me guiltily. "I didn't want to worry you, my beloved. It doesn't happen often. Only very strong lamassus can shift before birth."

I pinch the bridge of my nose. "My vagina is crying right now, Okot. It's never gonna be the same after that. *Never*. All those times I warned you about my narrow channel, well, now you've really done it. You've ruined it for good."

Evert takes our daughter from Okot's arms so that the midwife can hand the squirmy winged bull to him instead. The little bull sniffs Okot's fingers and nuzzles against his chest. It's little tail wags.

"I will gift you a token to show my love and appreciation

for the sacrifice you have made to your vagina," Okot tells me seriously.

"Okay. But I want a really, *really* good token. Like, the best freaking token *ever*. Better yet, I want two."

"It will be done, my beloved."

I nod tersely. "Good."

"I cannot believe you summoned me to see *that*," the demon whines, and I look over at him where he's slumped against the wall, sporting a black eye.

"It was an accident," I say.

"I never want to see that again."

I scowl. "I'll have you know that my vagina usually looks super appealing. You caught it at a bad time."

"It was like seeing a fleshy watermelon squeezing out of a fleshy oyster," he says with a shudder.

I glare at him. "Get out."

He nods. "Yes, ma'am."

With the snap of his fingers, he disappears in a puff of smoke. Sylred immediately opens the windows so the babies don't breathe any of it in.

My attention goes back to my lamassu mate and our son, who suddenly shifts from a bull to a baby boy. Okot wraps him in a blanket.

"Can I see them?" I ask.

"Of course you can," Ronak says, kissing me on the top of the head. "You did it, little demon."

I sigh in relief as Okot and Evert bring both babies up to me so I can see them. I start crying all over again as soon as my eyes land on their perfect little faces. "They're so tiny and beautiful," I say, placing a kiss on each of their cheeks. They've already fallen asleep, snuggled into their blankets.

"Twins," I say with wonder. "No wonder I was so big." I look at Okot. "I knew it was your fault."

Okot smiles shyly. I can tell he's proud, but he doesn't want to gloat since, you know, he's the reason I just had to push a bull out of my coochie.

"Umm, Emelle?" the midwife says.

My head swings over to face her.

And then another painful contraction hits.

She winces at my expression. "There's another baby."

CHAPTER 22

"*N*o!" I cry-scream. "No. I did two! I'm tapping out," I say, and I start tapping my hand against Ronak's face. "Tap! Tap me out! Someone tap me the fuck out! My turn is over!"

"You have to," the midwife says. "I already see the head."

"You made me give birth to a freaking litter!" I wail at Okot accusingly as a huge contraction takes over me.

I start sobbing uncontrollably, while Ronak and Sylred try to hold up my legs for me since I don't have the strength.

Sylred uses his Sound Soothe power to try to calm me down, but I'm so freaking exhausted and in pain that I don't know if I have it in me to do it for a third time.

Ronak must sense this, because he puts his alpha voice on. "Push, Emelle!"

"Fucking fine! AHHH!"

I push until I'm pretty sure I popped every blood vessel in my entire body. The last of my belly seems to deflate like a hot-air balloon with no more air, and the third baby comes out of me.

"Is it a freaking bull?" I pant weakly, totally collapsed against Sylred and Ronak. "Cuz I need so m-many tokennnss n-now, Okot. Y'hear meee?" I slur. I'm so exhausted I can't even speak.

The midwife holds up the baby—déjà vu—and I see another little girl. With my cupid wings and...a tail. A *genfin* tail.

My eyes snap to my genfins. "You...you. You got me pregnant...*while* I was already freaking *pregnant*!" I screech.

All three of them wince.

The midwife just chuckles. "It's very rare, but it can happen," she tells me.

I look at my mates murderously. "If there is another baby in me, so help me gods, I will literally smother you all in your sleep."

The midwife full out laughs at that. "No more babies, child. You're done. The afterbirths are already out," she says, clearly cleaning me up.

I glare again at my guys. "Did you hear that? The afterbirths are already out, and I barely felt it, because my vagina just pushed out three freaking babies, including a baby bull!"

The babies start crying, and I instantly feel bad. "Oh, I'm sorry, babies! Mommy's not mad at you. Mommy's mad at your daddies."

I open my arms for them, and very carefully, the guys hand me all three. I balance one in each arm, and let the third one nuzzle against my chest in the middle.

The midwife cleans everything up, including me, and then leaves, promising to check in again soon. Mossie brings Amorette home soon after, and when she sees three new babies instead of one, a new yellow flower pops out of her scalp. She plucks it for me and sets it on my nightstand.

"Thanks, Moss," I say around a yawn.

"So precious," she coos. "I'll babysit anytime. Except for nights. And seeding season. Or weeding Wednesdays."

"Of course."

When I yawn again, she quickly says her goodbyes and leaves so we can get some rest. It was a long, long labor, and I'm beat. Amorette crawled into Sylred's lap, and he's humming a low steady song, sending soothing waves of power out for our babies.

Good thing our bed is so big, because all nine of us are in it. Five adults and four kids, snuggled in together.

Each of my mates is holding one of our children. The sight is enough to make me teary-eyed. There's so much love in the room that my cupid boss mark is tingling against my skin.

I watch the guys as they gently rub the babies' backs and coo soft words to them, while little hands wrap around big fingers, and small noises of content escape their mouths. I can't contain my overwhelming joy, and every time I see the guys staring down at our babies with wonder and shining eyes, I get a bit choked up.

"I'm proud of you," Ronak says quietly as he cradles our new son.

Evert reaches forward and gently cups my jaw, landing a kiss on my lips. "So fucking proud, Scratch."

Okot is already asleep, our little bull daughter sleeping against his large chest, while Sylred continues to hum. Amorette is already fast asleep against him.

I thought I had all the love I'd ever get. But now? With all eight of them? My love is immeasurable.

"Triplets," I say, shaking my head in wonder. "Two cupid lamassus and a cupid genfin. Did that really just happen? It seems so perfectly impossible."

Sylred leans forward and kisses me on the top of my head. "But remember, love? You're always doing impossible things."

I smile. "That's because I knew."

"Knew what?" Ronak asks softly, careful not to wake any of our babies.

"That you all were worth every impossible thing," I reply tenderly.

Evert grins, both of his dimples coming out. "Happy Valentine's Day, Scratch."

I smile back. "Best Valentine's ever."

∼

The End

Enjoyed the Heart Hassle
Series?

Read on for the first chapter
in the stand-alone Heart
Hassle spin-off, *Sheer
Cupidity . . .*

WHICH BOOK WILL YOU READ NEXT?

CHAPTER 1

BELREN

I'm a master thief. Notorious for my ability to find anything anywhere.

I'm a collector of treasures and secrets, and in all the realm, fae know who the Horned Hook is, even if they've never seen my face without the horned mask.

So how the hell did I end up here, stuck in a cell during the middle of a fucking battle?

It's not ideal.

Battles are not my specialty. I don't go charging horns-first into violence. I'm much more of a stealthy, behind-the-curtains kind of male. I prefer stealing over stabbing.

"Hurry up," the black-haired genfin, Evert, growls as I use my telekinetic powers to break the chains off him and the other one—Sylred.

I cock a brow as the last of the iron chains fall away from their arms and legs, clunking against the splintery wooden walls. "A simple thank you would suffice."

"Thank you," Sylred quickly says, but he's the polite one, so it's expected.

He and Evert get up from the filthy dirt floor and stalk toward the entrance of this shitty makeshift cell we're in. Honestly, I'm insulted that the prince actually thought this partially underground hole could hold me. Although, it's better when people underestimate me. It's why I largely keep my telekinesis power under wraps. The pompous prince didn't have a clue.

The twat.

As soon as I think of Prince Elphar, I see red. I've been searching all over the realm for my sister, and then there Benicia was, under his control, completely at his mercy.

My sister has worked her entire life for the rebellion. She's wanted to make life better for the other fae since she could say the word *injustice*. But the prince found her and made her into a pawn. Somehow, he found out the connection between Benicia and his wife, Princess Soora.

Bile rises up my throat. Soora betrayed us. Betrayed me. She must've let something slip, and the prince used Benicia to blackmail Soora into her betrayal.

Rage simmers in my gut so hot that my skin feels as if it could blister.

I'm not sure who I hate more: the prince for what he's done or the princess for lying to me about my sister.

I could have helped Soora, thought of a way to get Benicia out, *and* still supported the rebellion. If only she had told me what was going on. Instead, she chose to betray us all.

"Are you fucking pulling on your dick over there? Let's go," Evert hisses, making my attention flick to him. Sylred doesn't chastise him. I know they're a bit uptight about their cupid mate possibly being in danger, but I have half a mind to snap my fingers and put the chains back around him. At the very least, a gag would be nice.

"Fuck off."

They both crouch against the wood-slatted wall, trying to peer through slivers of light at the boarded ceiling. They're probably counting the number of guards that are outside. Amateurs.

With a roll of my eyes, I break the iron lock from the door and make it go careening out, using the force of it to smack into one of the guards. The other two are quickly overpowered by Sylred and Evert, knocked unconscious, and all three tossed into the room we just escaped from.

I slam the door shut with a twist of my wrist, and then the lock floats back up and clicks into place.

"There, was that quick enough for you?" I challenge before making the last of Evert's broken chains still stuck around his ankles fall away.

Before he can answer, a cupid suddenly pops into existence in front of us mid-run, holding a bow and arrow.

Lex.

My eyes are immediately riveted to her as she hurries toward us. "I've been looking everywhere for you," she says to the genfins.

Evert and Sylred startle at her appearance, but quickly tense up again when they realize it's not *their* cupid. "Where's Emelle?" Evert asks.

Lex points in the direction she came from. "She's over there. She sent me to look for you, and—"

A huge boom sounds, making all of us drop to our haunches as the ground vibrates with the force.

"What the fuck was that?" Evert calls, looking around

the island, though our view is blocked with another shoddy building just in front of us.

My ears are ringing, and magic practically spits in the air, making me grit my teeth. Whatever the fuck that was, it was strong.

"We have angels and demons fighting with us now," Lex says, delicate hand clenching her bow, and the sight makes my heart race with nerves. If I'm not suited for battles, then she *definitely* isn't. Especially with her ridiculous human clothes. I'm not even sure how she runs in that skirt or how the buttons on her blouse still look so shiny.

"You shouldn't be here," I growl as I get to my feet and grip her arm to help her stand back up.

"I had to find Madame Cupid's mates," she tells me, and I can't help noticing how good she smells. Like sugar and...paper? Weird combination, but alright. "And I'm perfectly safe in the Veil."

"Yes, but you're not *in* the Veil right now," I point out.

"Well, of course I'm not, or you wouldn't be able to see me," she snips back, sounding annoyed. For some reason, her tone makes my eyes latch onto her pretty pink lips, and I have the rushing urge to lean down and nibble them.

Well, I do enjoy beautiful, unique things, so it's really no surprise that I seem to be infatuated with her. I knew I was intrigued by cupids when Emelle stumbled into my life, but the second I laid eyes on Lex, I was entranced.

She's so deliciously *proper*. I want to peel back that high-necked blouse and see how *improper* I can make her.

"Cover my back," Evert says to Sylred. "I'm going to

check the building in front of us, and then we're getting to our mate."

Sylred nods, and we watch as Evert rushes to the slipshod building and skirts around the edge, disappearing from sight just as another loud noise blares out. I glance up to see a burst of flames shooting through the sky.

I quickly pull Lex against the side of the building where we have somewhat more cover. "Go back into the Veil where it's safe. This is no place for a cupid."

She shoves a stray piece of hair behind her ear. "I'll have you know that I once made twelve Love Matches during a human war."

My eyes widen. "Don't you dare try to make Love Matches right now, Sixty-Nine."

"My name is Lex," she says primly, trying to cover up the Roman numeral cupid mark on the inside of her wrist. "And I will make a Match whenever the opportunity arises."

A growl of frustration rumbles through my chest. "*Pinky.* Get out of here."

Is she *trying* to get herself hurt? She's got pink nails for gods' sake. She shouldn't be here, vulnerable like this. What was Emelle thinking?

I decide right then and there that Lex needs someone looking out for her, and when this is over, I'm going to woo the shit out of her to assure her that *I'm* that someone.

One of our first discussions needs to be about the importance of reading a room. Or in this case, a literal *battlefield*.

Just as she opens her mouth no doubt to argue about the importance of spreading love even during dangerous times or some shit, her cupid mark glows. She shoots me a look, and then disappears in a cloud of pink.

I finally let out the breath that was tightening my chest.

When the smoke clears, I see Sylred smirking. "I know that look."

Yep. Should've gagged them. "Shut it."

Just then, Evert rushes back over with a few more droplets of blood on him than he had before. I don't think it's his. "The building is clear. Let's go."

Together, the three of us sprint from our hidden spot between the buildings, and step out into absolute fucking mayhem.

High fae and genfins are fighting on the ground and in the sky, power being wielded just as much as swords. We dodge it as much as we can, because Evert and Sylred's sole focus is getting back to their mate.

Mine is finding my sister.

The battle is a fucking mess.

Lex wasn't kidding, either. There are some males and females battling for us that are definitely *not* fae. If the black- or white-feathered wings didn't give them away, it's the sheer power that they emanate. I guess the cupids have a lot of pull to get actual demons and angels to come here and help us win this fight. And considering the fire spurts and blasts of light, I'm very glad we have them on our side.

The further the three of us run into the fray, the more fighting we have to dodge or block. Evert and Sylred don't have weapons, but *I'm* a weapon, which means the majority of it is up to me.

They should be very glad they have *me* on their side.

Left and right, above us and in front, I use my powers to knock fae out of the way and give us a clear path without myself or the genfins getting hurt. Emelle would probably shoot a Love Arrow through my balls if I let anything happen to them.

I do sort of owe her for saving my life.

Plus, I like her and her mates. Not that I would ever admit such a thing out loud.

But the battle, even if I'm just actively making it avoid us, is taking its toll on me. The more fae or weapons I have to send flying away, the weaker I become. Sweat is dripping down my back, it's hard to take a full breath, and my vision is going a little tunnelled. It's draining, having my senses on a swivel, trying to make sure no one sneaks up on us from any angle.

All the while, I'm searching for any glimpse of my sister or Soora, but they're not here in the fray.

I need to find Benicia...

I feel myself growing weaker, but I can't afford to hold back. I keep using my magic, not letting a single bastard catch us unawares. And plenty of the high fae come for us. With glazed, almost unseeing eyes, they try to hack at us with their swords anytime we come into their path. Knowing they're in full mind-control mode, I try my best to send them careening away or to yank the weapons from their grips instead of wounding them fatally.

With this much fighting going on, running across the field takes so much longer than it should. I don't catch every attack. Evert gets a fist of a high fae to the back of his head, and Sylred gets laid out by a wayward burst of ice power.

But I get us across the damn field, and that's what

matters. Unfortunately, I'm about ready to drop from exhaustion by the time we do, and still, no Benicia.

Where is she?

"It's winding down!" Evert shouts, and just as he says it, I'm able to shake my head and really take in the entire scene around us, instead of just the possible nearby threats. I didn't even notice that there aren't as many swords clashing or screams sounding until just now. The battle is definitely slowing.

With the angels and demons giving us aid, the genfins have gained the upper hand. I watch as a huge group of high fae are knocked unconscious with bouts of bright power coming from the angels, and another group is rounded up in a giant ring of fire by the demons.

There are still far too many fae dead littering the ground, but at least some of the high fae can be spared. It's not their fault we have a fucked-up monarchy.

"You okay?" Sylred asks me, hand on my shoulder.

I didn't even realize I was swaying.

"Fine," I say, shrugging him off.

He's frowning at me, but then his eyes shift to somewhere behind me. "There she is!"

Evert and I both turn our gazes, latching onto Emelle's pink hair.

"Fucking finally," Evert grits out, and I hear the stark relief in his tone.

But me? I'm not relieved. Because there is a *second* pink-haired female standing right there with her. Lex is standing beside Emelle, clearly *not* in the Veil, looking out of place and deliciously rumpled.

This just solidifies my previous thought. She *definitely* needs my protection. Or maybe I should put her over my lap and punish her for putting herself in danger *again* after I explicitly told her to stay in the Veil.

Evert and Sylred hurry over to reunite with Emelle and their two other covey members, Ronak and Okot, who are already with her.

Gods, she has a lot of mates.

My eyes stay latched onto Lex as I stalk over. As if she can feel me looking, her head turns and she locks onto me. She doesn't even have the forethought to pretend to look contrite.

Little minx.

She looks away, pretending to be aloof, but I smirk when I see the blush that stains her cheeks.

Oh, Pinky. Just you wait 'til I get you alone.

I'll have her blushing from head to toe, and show her exactly why she shouldn't put herself in danger. She might try to play this detached, innocent cupid, but I know better. There's something under that exterior that calls to me.

When she steals another quick glance my way, my lips curve. With that one look, something inside me just solidified.

I'm going to make her mine.

I don't know where the thought comes from, but as soon as it forms in my head, it's done, decided. I *will* do this.

Not as a conquest, either. Sure, there will be a chase and a catch, but I'm going to keep her. Perhaps Emelle came into my life not only to save it, but to lead me to Lex. The fates like to play funny games like that.

This new vow rushes through my veins and holds steady in my chest, like it's simply been waiting for me to acknowledge it. I can feel it with all-consuming determination as I watch the red-winged beauty who's now wringing her hands in front of her. Does she know I'm about to go on the hunt? Can she feel it? I have more adrenaline and excitement pumping in me than I've had in a long time. It's the old familiar rush that comes when I go for something truly momentous as a master thief.

I've stolen a lot of things in my life. Treasures. People. Secrets.

But now? I'm going for the most precious thing of all.

I'm going to steal this cupid's heart.

The distraction of this groundbreaking revelation costs me a precious second as I rip my gaze away from her in order to see that several feet away, Prince Elphar himself is being restrained by a couple of massive angels.

The fucker.

My fists curl, and I consider walking over there to punch him in the face for what he did to Benicia. It would feel good to get out a bit of this aggression the old-fashioned way, especially since I don't think I could do anything with my magic right now while I'm so depleted.

But I don't get the chance at any kind of revenge.

In less time than it takes to blink, the prince shoves out a massive blast of power, knocking down everyone nearby with the wrath of his magic.

The breath gets sucked out of me as I land flat on my back, my skull rattled and my back barking with pain. For a moment, I can't move, but then I finally manage to roll onto my stomach and push myself up. Before I can get to my feet though, I hear his bone-chilling shout that makes every hair on the back of my neck lift up.

"CUPID!"

He's furious. Enraged. Emelle has not only cost him this battle, but the entire war against the monarchy. He can never come back from this, and he knows it. All of that is relayed in this single shout he roars. He wants to make her pay.

My neck snaps up, and I see that Emelle is still down from the blast of power, her body smashed against the dirt, but Lex is up and trying to help her up. Lex's back is to the prince, pink hair loose and red wings on full display.

Horror washes over me when I realize that the prince's attention has latched onto the wrong cupid.

Lex.

Terror bursts in my chest when I see wicked light gather in his palm, and then he *throws it.*

I don't have time to think or breathe or blink. I don't even have the time to try to scrape together the last of my own magic and shove him away, because he's already released the power, and it's not something physical that I can control. So I'm forced to watch in horrifying slow-motion as it hurtles straight at *my* cupid.

No.

My body is up and moving before I even feel the pump of my legs. I jump in front of her without hesitation.

I'm not sure what happens first—my feet landing on the ground or the power hitting me square in the chest. It's hard to say, because all I feel in the next instant is blinding, insurmountable agony.

It hits me so quickly that I don't have the luxury of seeing my life pass before my eyes. And what does a thief really have to be proud of anyway in his last moments?

But the prince's magic crashes into me instead of Lex, and that's what matters.

The last thing I see as I'm thrown down on my back, as the power shatters my bones and explodes my insides, is her blurry form.

Pink hair, red wings.

And all I can think is, I wish I'd had more time.

But I guess even a master thief can't steal that.

CHAPTER 2

BELREN

here's nothing.

There is a grimy whiteness all around that is neither light nor shadow, cool nor warm. There is no land or water or air. I have no body. No sense of touch. No recollection of what came before or if anything is coming after.

But there is one thing in the nothing.

One single, solitary thing that I remember.

Her.

Red wings, serious face, pink hair pulled back tight.

I have no idea who she was. But I remember her in this nothingness.

I don't know how long I'm stuck in this strange existence. Maybe seconds. Maybe decades. Maybe I'm not here at all, and this is all a dream. But then suddenly, the nothingness shifts. And then I feel a *pull*.

I'm yanked out of this ether of nothing, and the next thing I know, I blink into being.

Confused and shaking, I look down, realizing that I

can look, and see a body. *My* body. I raise my silver hands in front of my face, and then carefully touch my cheeks. Except I don't feel a thing.

My fingers go through me, and I pull them back to study them again, and realize that they're slightly see-through.

"What…"

My voice sounds hoarse and loud, and not familiar at all.

Who am I?

Where am I?

"Next!"

My head jerks up, and I blink at the sight before me. I'm in a large room, and there are lots of other…translucent bodies around me.

All shapes, sizes, colors, sexes, and I can't be sure if I recognize any of them or not, because I don't even recognize myself.

"Next!" the voice calls out again, sounding irritated.

I look ahead again, only to realize that I'm actually standing in line. Based on the winged female sitting at the desk and glaring at me, I'd say that I'm next, and I'm wasting her time.

I step forward, but *this* translucent body doesn't actually step. It takes some finagling, but I manage to float forward until I'm standing before her.

"You're here to be processed."

I blanch. "What? What does that mean?"

She points to the brochures that are presented on her desk. One of them has an angel on it with the slogan "Were you good in life? Well, now you can be great!"

My eyes dart to the next brochure over, and I see a

picture of a black-winged demon with the words "Like it sizzling hot? Come down under for a good time!" When I lean in closer, I read the fine print that says "*Some torturing may apply" underneath.

I frown and look back up at the female. "What is this?"

Sighing, she gives me a look that says she's been asked to explain this far too many times for her liking. And judging by the length of the line behind me, I suppose she has.

"Welcome to the afterlife," she drawls. "Time to pick your new job."

Want more of Raven Kennedy?

Check out the phenomenal and addictive Plated Prisoner Series.

A fantasy retelling of the notorious King Midas myth, with a dark and magical twist . . .

And the final epic chapter in the series . . .

GOLD coming December 2023

He just wanted a decent book to read ...

Not too much to ask, is it? It was in 1935 when Allen Lane, Managing Director of Bodley Head Publishers, stood on a platform at Exeter railway station looking for something good to read on his journey back to London. His choice was limited to popular magazines and poor-quality paperbacks – the same choice faced every day by the vast majority of readers, few of whom could afford hardbacks. Lane's disappointment and subsequent anger at the range of books generally available led him to found a company – and change the world.

'We believed in the existence in this country of a vast reading public for intelligent books at a low price, and staked everything on it'
Sir Allen Lane, 1902–1970, founder of Penguin Books

The quality paperback had arrived – and not just in bookshops. Lane was adamant that his Penguins should appear in chain stores and tobacconists, and should cost no more than a packet of cigarettes.

Reading habits (and cigarette prices) have changed since 1935, but Penguin still believes in publishing the best books for everybody to enjoy. We still believe that good design costs no more than bad design, and we still believe that quality books published passionately and responsibly make the world a better place.

So wherever you see the little bird – whether it's on a piece of prize-winning literary fiction or a celebrity autobiography, political tour de force or historical masterpiece, a serial-killer thriller, reference book, world classic or a piece of pure escapism – you can bet that it represents the very best that the genre has to offer.

Whatever you like to read – trust Penguin.